MONSIGNOR WILLIAM BARRY MEMORIAL LIBRARY
BARRY UNIVERSITY
PS3551.S54 S3
Asinof, Eliot, 1919- cn   010101 000
Say it ain't so, Gordon Little

0 2210 0061132 9

Y0-CJF-849

PS
3551   163883
.S54
S3

Msgr. Wm. Barry Memorial Library
Barry University
Miami Shores, FL   33161

ASINOF

SAY IT AIN'T SO...

Say It Ain't So, Gordon Littlefield

Books by Eliot Asinof

Man on Spikes
Eight Men Out
The Bedfellow
Seven Days to Sunday
The Name of the Game Is Murder
People v. Blutcher
Craig and Joan
The Ten Second Jail Break
   (with Warren Hinckle and William Turner)
The Fox Is Crazy Too

Say It Ain't So, Gordon Littlefield

a novel by

ELIOT ASINOF

E. P. DUTTON
NEW YORK

Copyright © 1977 by Eliot Asinof
All rights reserved. Printed in the U.S.A.

No part of this publication may be reproduced or transmitted in any form or by any means, electronic or mechanical, including photocopy, recording or any information storage and retrieval system now known or to be invented, without permission in writing from the publisher, except by a reviewer who wishes to quote brief passages in connection with a review written for inclusion in a magazine, newspaper or broadcast.

Library of Congress Cataloging in Publication Data

Asinof, Eliot
  Say it ain't so, Gordon Littlefield.
  I. Title.
PZ4.A832Say3   [PS3551.S54]   813'.5'4   77–1608

ISBN: 0-525-19610-2

Published simultaneously in Canada by Clarke, Irwin & Company Limited, Toronto and Vancouver

10 9 8 7 6 5 4 3 2 1

First Edition

Say It Ain't So,
Gordon Littlefield

THE NEW YORK BULLS

OFFENSE:

Quarterback	Jackson, Thomas J. "Stonewall"
Halfback	Carter, Loren "Ace"
Fullback	Zoad, Edmund "Z"
Flanker	Barone, Coleman
Wide Receiver	Warner, Gil
Left Tackle	Hoover, Samuel "Buck"
Left Guard	Baletti, Gino
Center	Noren, Charles
Right Guard	Stover, Perry Lee
Right Tackle	Browne, Merrill
Tight End	Jones, Willie
Kicker	Grazlov, Vassily

DEFENSE:

Right End	Payson, Monroe "Sonny"
Right Tackle	Bow, Lem
Left Tackle	Henderson, Alex
Left End	LaTourette, John "Tiny"
Right Linebacker	Wisting, Etore
Middle Linebacker	Kling, Judson
Left Linebacker	Kolacka, Jake
Right Cornerback	Coll, Henry
Left Cornerback	Snyder, Ernest
Free Safety	Ayers, Oscar
Strong Safety	St. Clair, Rolland

HEAD COACH: Ike Seager
ORTHOPEDIC SURGEON: Dr. Paul Knowland
TRAINER: Nat Repple
PRESS SECRETARY: Ed Mann
EQUIPMENT MANAGER: Sy Getz

1
Prologue

I am not one who generally suffers fits of nervousness. A placid man, educated in the finest traditions of dispassion and poise. Furthermore, a man with experience of an exceptionally varied nature, frequently not without a flare for high drama. At this instant, however, I find myself shaking uncontrollably.

Let me explain. This is the Superbowl. The Los Angeles Coliseum. A huge marching band stands elegantly in the center of the field. Rival championship teams wait on the sidelines accompanied by coaches, trainers, assistants, media photographers as the speakers bellow: "Ladies and gentlemen, our National Anthem." I stand as rigidly as I can, my feet straddling the sideline as I face the distant flagpole, visored cap in right hand reverently over my heart. But as I begin to mouth those austere lyrics, my throat locks, demanding more lubrication than I can generate. I find myself gasping for air with heaving chest, desperately attempting to sing though I can barely move my lips. I am now doubly conscious of the television cameras, for the transistor radio in my shirt pocket already referred to my presence when I first walked on the field ("... and there, carrying a load of towels, is the celebrated writer Gordon Littlefield, currently preparing a new book as waterboy for the New York Bulls ..."). Though I try to minimize the possibility that any camera, much less the chosen one, will be concentrating on me, I have visions of an opportunistic TV director in front of his monitor taking his pleasure at my expense, and 90,000,000 viewers will be asking themselves: "Why isn't Littlefield singing? *Doesn't he know the words?*" Like a fool, I steal a peripheral glance for the telltale red light above the camera lens, then quickly abort this maneuver, remembering how vulnerable one appears on screen at such moments—all of which induce a fresh wave of anxiety that beads my face with instant perspiration.

But only for a moment, to be sure. Even as I succumb to these fears, I am aware of their transiency. After all, such tension is perfectly normal under the circumstances. Like stage fright with an actor on opening night. Indeed, I have no real cause for concern, having worked out all necessary details. I have but to do my simple chores and enjoy the afternoon's fulfillment.

My mind shifts then from panic to anticipated ecstasy, my body stands tall and elegantly at rest. I can now regard the flag fluttering in the breeze with a burst of pride. Old Glory, yes. It is really quite magnificent, a colorful sight against the bright blue-white sky. The trumpets reverberate through the huge arena in stirring bombast, a dozen big bass drums are pounding as one, and those hearty American voices resound in tribute to "broad stripes and bright stars." While I am no flag-waving jingoist, I cannot help but react, and the back of my neck literally tingles.

It is the enormity of what I have done that stirs me. I sense I am standing totally alone in this multitude, for on this day I shall witness the consummation of what may well be the most unique sporting event in modern history.

Or, as some may prefer to call it, the unfolding of a perfect crime. Most gratifying to me, however, is the awareness that I am doubtless the only man alive who could possibly bring it off.

For I, Gordon Littlefield III, have actually *fixed* the Superbowl game.

2

Monday (Thirteen Days to Go)

Let me pose the obvious question: how does a man from a distinguished heritage dating back to the arrival of the Mayflower itself; whose family traditions were of the ultimate respectability; whose career was marked by an almost unbroken chain of literary and social triumphs; whose personal life was regarded by all as the apogee of glamour, exquisite taste and discernment—how does such a man come to this incredible act?

The answer, of course, is hardly a simple one. One notes the passage in *The Great Gatsby* wherein Scott Fitzgerald's narrator has supposed that the famous fixing of the 1919 World Series came about as "a thing that merely happened, the end of some inevitable chain" not the manipulation of one individual "with the singlemindedness of a burglar blowing a safe." Actually, the Black Sox Scandal, as it came to be called, indicates that the former notion is the more accurate one. In this instance, however, I suggest a combination of Fitzgerald's alternatives. If this Superbowl game was fixed by one person, myself, my involvement derived from the impact of a simple, special date.

December 29, to be exact. For on that auspicious day, I became forty years old.

I awakened on that chilly morning, stared at the rococo ceiling of my spacious bedroom on New York's fashionable East 64th Street in lugubrious catatonia, having suffered an endless night shuttling from my bed to the cold commode. I had never had such a reaction to any previous birthday, either after all the cake and ice cream of my pampered adolescence or the champagne of my glittering manhood. I am—and always have been—a healthy animal, never having suffered from headaches or hives or even colds. But in the face of psychic trauma, I confess an acute sensitivity with my digestive process, the epicenter of my lean 6'2" frame. The stomach as Achilles Heel.

Arriving at this awesome date, I suddenly saw myself differently. I didn't know why it should have affected me, for it was downright silly to think there was really anything significant about any birthday or any age. Was it not merely one day after the day before? What ridiculous mystique bid so many of us to take note of these passing decades as though all of life were to be placed in certain tightly circumscribed segments? Could not A at thirty actually be considerably "older" than B at forty?

Nonetheless, I found myself trapped by the very mores I knew enough to reject, as helpless as a child terrorized by a monster film. Naturally, I battled with my senses in a vain attempt to rally, reminding myself that reality was far more glorious. After all, I was quite good-looking in an open, boyish manner. My brown eyes shone with a 20-20 clarity and my brown hair had neither receded nor greyed. I looked considerably like a young prince in his prime—or so others thought of me—the logical outgrowth of my heritage. A graduate of Princeton, '56, though neither genius nor star athlete, what I lacked in talent was compensated by my affability. If my prime achievement was less than stellar (assistant editor on the *Daily Princetonian*) I was nonetheless designated as The Man Most Likely to Succeed, an extravagant prediction that turned out to be entirely valid. I had left college with high aspirations in politics, perhaps, with an eye toward alleviating the injustices of American society: racism, poverty, war, the usual *bête noires* of humanitarians. Instead, I stumbled into a writer-editor's job on a new chic magazine in New York's prestigious world of media and quickly found a métier that appeared to suit my personality. It began as a whim of mine, a notion to perform as a rather bumbling amateur along with great professionals, then write the all too humbling experience of the contrast. Luckily, I was able to convince the Harlem Globetrotters —that unique collection of black basketball players—to include this less than talented white whose abilities in this sport never exceeded second string at prep school (Choate). My spastic performance before a few thousand South Jerseyites on the converted stage of a motion picture theater lasted barely six minutes and I was more hooted than laughed at. But when I wrote of it, I created a style that reversed this negative reaction, and my readers found the article both comedic and informative.

I followed this with what appeared to be a conspicuous show of bravery, marching alone into a circus cage in the black boots and britches of a lion tamer, whip in one hand, wooden chair in the other, sidearms holstered on my hip. The lion, of course, had been drugged to a semistupor, the sole justification for my grandiose gestures of contempt; when he managed even a semblance of a toothy grunt, however, I went tumbling over backward, the whip entwining my legs to immobilize me, enhancing my terror.

I then joined a roller derby, ostensibly subjecting myself to its chaotic violence, though actually completely protected by an agreement among all participants that no harm would befall me—a pact that was duplicated by professional hockey players when I performed briefly as goalie in an NHL exhibition game.

It all seemed harmless enough, though I confess that the literary accolades thrown my way were far greater than I anticipated. What had begun with whimsy became something of a symbol, quite overblown at that, for it was written of me that I actually risked life and limb, daring to go where others would not. And if I fumbled and failed, these were Everyman's failures, and in contrast with the skills of professionals, my experiences then proved reassuring to all.

So it was that I'd found a career that made me something of a legend before I was thirty. Gimmicky, perhaps, and opportunistic, and infinitely more beneficial to Gordon Littlefield than the alleviation of those above-mentioned injustices, nevertheless it could be said that I'd brought pleasure to my readers by living out their own fantasies. In short, I could be proud of my accomplishment.

Also, as a celebrity of sorts, I was invited everywhere. I dined with United States presidents, partied with motion picture stars and their potentates, hunted flesh of all kinds with leading athletes all over the world. My life became such a literary, theatrical, sporting and romantic party, it was written of me that "this glamorous bachelor has become the envy of every American male."

Then why, at forty, was I so severely shaken? If I can explain little, I nonetheless assume it reveals a lot. One thing seems certain: it was not mere coincidence that the commitment to fix the Superbowl was initiated on this auspicious birthday.

It had seemed safest to remain in bed. I was not one to be sensitive to the paths of the moon or fascinated by messages derived from tarot cards, but I had an ominous feeling that any experience on that day would tend to overwhelm me. Even the telephone became an enemy, and when it rang, I burrowed under the bedclothes until my answering service could intervene. I absolutely refused to answer the doorbell. Survival seemed to lie in complete reclusion.

When I managed to work my way out of bed, it was more out of the pressures of my bladder than any relaxation of turmoil. While the coffee brewed, I dared to check for telephone messages, somewhat relieved to discover nothing more sanguine than a call from one agent who handles my TV and magazine commercials (I sip Royal British Tea in a maroon tuxedo and comment on the "maleness" of its texture and taste), and another who books me on an occasional lecture tour. (I was scheduled to speak at three Southern colleges for women on successive nights in April.) I turned to the morning *Times* and was immediately trapped by the front page stories of the New York Bulls and yesterday's playoff victory. It was easy enough to understand the city's enthusiasm, for this was the first New York football championship since 1969 and the Jets of early Joe Willie Namath.

But it left me cold. Despite all my affinity for the sporting scene, I viewed this triumph with considerable disdain. I was not a Bulls fan. I did not like the coarse, brutal cast of the team, its helter-skelter style, its chaotic bent. I liked my football more scientific and orderly, more directed toward artistry than mayhem. Above all, I could not stomach the man who owned the team—indeed, who created it in his vulgar image—an emotion sufficient to overwhelm any possible détente with my above-mentioned prejudices. His name was Lester Stillson, about whom more, much more, will follow.

Suffice to say, all this bode ill, that my birthday thoughts should turn so early in the morning to so loathsome a character. They could not but stoke the fires of my discontent, feeding my anxiety in a clumsy self-destructive cycle. It was a morning which presumably demanded nothing of me, yet I felt totally incapable of enjoying it. I found myself caught between Scylla (do something!) and Charybdis (be wary!), both of which intimidated me.

In the end, I opted for Scylla.

After a second cup of coffee and two slices of toasted English muffins, I could be proud of a now tranquil stomach. A false sense of security, perhaps, but sufficient to inspire a venture into the outside world. A healthy release, it would be. A visit to my athletic club for a game of squash.

3

A number of important people congregated several times a week at the Knickerbocker A.C., for the primary purpose of meeting other important people. I sensed a comparable need in myself, and therefore saw it clearly in others. I also enjoyed the workouts, in fact, relied on them for the perpetuation of a youthful posture. I could even call it a tax-deductible professional obligation as important to my career as a variety of literary subscriptions or throwing parties for distinguished guests.

Monday was always a big day, and by mid-afternoon the locker room was crowded with a need to sweat out the overindulgences of the winter weekend. Also typical was the Monday talk of football, especially relating to the champion New York Bulls—all the more intimately since Lester Stillson himself was a member.

I let it flow around me, all this adolescent jabber from the mouths of America's tycoons: a pair of young millionaire stockbrokers, a corporation lawyer with White House connections, an advertising executive, a magazine publisher. The power people, tastemakers, the elite, all fascinated by the Bulls like a covey of children at a high school pep rally. The new democracy at work—one dialogue for everyone.

I undressed slowly, concentrating on the comings and goings that I might best select a squash rival. I was about to approach the corporation lawyer, an agreeable competitor with a steady, stylish game, but he opted for a sauna and massage. I was standing naked in my socks when the unmistakable voice of Lester Stillson came bursting in with the modesty of a Hell's Angel on a Saturday night in Oakland.

"Well, you bastards, I told you so! . . ."

And so he had. He was merely the owner of the Bulls but he entered as though he owned the world, pausing in the doorway for a second or two of gloating pomposity.

He was not the handsomest of men by any means. His head was considerably larger than it ought to be ("swelled," as a million columnists had put it), and his nose was canted somewhat awkwardly to add a devious quality to the already unappealing face. A small mouth with thin lips only partially masked by a sprawling moustache. Wiry black hair turning grey. Beady blue eyes encased in large horn-rimmed glasses. He was a natty dresser, always in jarring color and flare. Bold, the fashion people would say of his taste, obviously calculated to draw attention to himself, for when you looked at Lester Stillson, Lester Stillson knew you weren't looking elsewhere.

He was a small man, no more than 5'6". He moved quickly with jerky, uncoordinated moves as though he were offering a minimal target lest some enemy choose to draw a bead on him. (I was told that he always sat in restaurants with his back to the wall—like gangsters in old movies.) Currently in his late forties, he took to gathering fat, especially around his middle, forming a rather strange contour below his overlarge head that suggested a double-dip ice cream cone.

There was, however, nothing confectionary about his history. He had a genius for making enemies and surviving them. Even the press (in a secret ballot) voted him the Unpopularity Award. His talent for exploitation was legendary. He had loyalties to no one and related to nothing but his self-interest. There were no traditions he respected. When it came to acquiring new players, he broke as many rules as he needed to, then settled for half when he had to—which was half more than he deserved. He lied to his coaches, humiliated his players, cheated his fans. He did business like an old robber baron, but when his club began to win, he begged, bought, threatened his way to a good press to glorify his image. (They ended up calling him a "Millionaire Maverick.")

It was incredible the way he won. He won everything from a battle with a supply company over an alleged shortage of a few dozen towels to a court action over his tampering with another club's quarterback. He won close games in the final seconds on the flukes of a football bounce or the arbitrary decision of a referee in a blinding snowstorm. He won more and more, and he never stopped talking about it, relating every victory to something he had done. He would leak stories to writers on his payroll, always taking the credit for such unorthodox plays as a fake punt in the first quarter that kept a drive going, or a daring end-around on his own one yard line that went for fifty-five yards.

"The world of professional football smells," wrote a feisty sportswriter named Joe Weed, "but Lester makes it putrid."

He must have sensed my hostile stare, for he turned from his locker and challenged me.

"Littlefield, I'll whip your Princeton ass on the squash court."

I smiled. Though I had never seen him play, I doubted his talent, visualizing one of those pitiful one-sided games wherein I got very little workout. Still, this was the indomitable Lester Stillson and it might prove enjoyable to tantalize the worm.

"Why, certainly, Lester. I'll try to defend Princeton's honor."

He was already plunging into the business of undressing, tearing off shirt and tie as though they were on fire. In fact, he ended up lacing his sneakers a few seconds ahead of me.

Then came the question that threatened to alter history: "Well, Littlefield, how do you like my boys?"

I suppose I could have sloughed it off with an appropriate compliment. After all, he *had* built a winner, all expert predictions to the contrary. Perhaps it was the nature of the day, or my less than tranquil mood, or the presence of so many others, or, simply, my antipathy toward this man. My reply came from the stomach, not the brain.

"To be frank with you, Lester, I would say that they're a highly overrated team."

"You'd say what!??"

"It constantly amazes me that the Bulls keep winning —all too frequently by extraordinary luck."

There was a small truth in what I was saying though I'd hate to have to defend it among experts. In front of this little popinjay, however, the words hit like poisoned darts.

"What bullshit!" he barked.

The room took on the silence of high drama. Having dug myself in, at least I could shovel some dirt on *him*.

"Lester, you're blinded by your enthusiasm."

"I thought we just won the championship," he snarled. "Of course, if I'm blind, maybe I read the scoreboard wrong."

Quick laughter from the benches, and I waited a beat to reply, but Lester compounded his little victory with an instant replay.

"We *did* win, didn't we?"

More laughter. Another beat. All eyes were on me again. My attention turned to my squash racket, testing the tension in its strings, gut rapping against heel-of-hand. When I looked up, I tried for all the boyishness I could put into a smile.

"Lester, I believe that Dallas will wipe you out in the Superbowl."

It was as if I'd shot him right between the eyes. You could see him wince as the bullet hit, bringing on a sinister curl to his moustache. Curiously, he had nothing to say in rebuttal as everyone waited, all movement stalled for the duration. His large head was jutting from his neck like a fighter daring to be slugged.

"Littlefield . . ." he began, slurring the three syllables of my name into a profane reading. "I've never seen you play this game . . . for all I know you may be the greatest squash player who ever stepped on a goddam court. But to me you're an asshole and, by Jesus, I can beat an asshole like you at *anything*." Then, charged up by his own rage, he spit out his challenge: "I'll even bet you a thousand bucks I'm right!"

For an audience of about ten, this was not a bad show. I felt the impact of their anticipation and assumed a properly cavalier attitude.

"Well, I can assure you, Lester, I'm far from the greatest. . . ." I could hardly contain a smile. "A thousand dollars, then."

And so the battle was joined. History will judge it as a prelude to the Superbowl itself. Others hurriedly rearranged their schedules (at least two rushed to the telephone to forestall business appointments). Everything came to a standstill as we two titans began to tangle.

Strange, this sudden brouhaha, fabricated out of what now seemed to be absolutely nothing, and definitely not my style. I had lived a life without controversy, avoiding hostilities at all costs as a matter of temperament. Aggression was poor policy and bad for the psyche. If I had been successful in my career, it was due to friendships, not animosities. Yet, here I was with a pugnacious stance, having allowed an improper emotion to guide my tongue —if not like an anus than surely like a fool.

It was all connected with my birthday blues, no doubt. Then I began hitting the squash ball and promptly forgot everything else.

I was relieved to see that Lester was as inept as he was arrogant, perhaps as much as eight points my inferior in the fifteen-point game. I was also quick to see that this differential did not appear to bother him at all. He moved awkwardly, swung wildly, did not know where to go and how to get there, but he played with the feel of one who believed exactly the opposite. Was this pure bullish ignorance, or did it suggest some subtle quality of the man himself? Whatever, I would take pleasure in beating him with minimum effort, gracefully, without vindictiveness —exactly the way I preferred to do everything. If I had to despise this man, I saw no reason to end up despising myself.

I was, after all, at home on the court, having played this game steadily since my days at Princeton though not with any competitive zeal. It was more typical of me to enjoy merely stroking the shots properly as though winning were irrelevant. On this day, however, I was anything but lackadaisical, taking control of the game right from its inception. If, at times, I found pleasure merely keeping the ball in play, I knew I could put it away whenever I wished. I was leading 9–4 when I confronted what would have to be called the first signs of trouble: I'd made three points in a row, then finally missed a shot, and Stillson moved into the service box, announcing the score at 8–5.

"I beg your pardon, Lester. I'm certain I have 9."

He did not even reply, and with complete contempt for my claim, hit his service.

"Lester . . ." I began again, ignoring the service. "The score is 9–4."

"Don't give me that. I can count. You had six when you began serving. I remember that distinctly. I said it out loud."

"Correct. I then made three straight points."

"Two. You made two!" he barked, assuming a ridiculous adolescent posture as he appealed to the gallery.

"Three, Lester," returned the consensus.

"All right, all right," he conceded. "9–5."

And immediately he began serving again as my brain recorded the "5" as a second discrepancy of numbers, leaving me to speculate on whether to contest that too, and before I could shake its impact, he had made three quick points himself.

He was playing with a fresh ferocity now, his awkwardness leading to occasional body contact, at one point, exactly as I was swinging. Not surprisingly, I missed the shot.

"9–8!" he cried out.

Customarily, a "let" is called on such interference, and the point is replayed. Not at all certain that I wanted another skirmish, however, especially since the others appeared to enjoy the new closeness of the score, I let it pass, never doubting my eventual victory. I had barely returned to my receiving area when the ball came bounding at my feet, and again, I missed the return.

"9–all!" he roared, well before I could protest his quick service, then adding with a supercilious grin: "That is correct, is it not?" loudly imitating my own broad manner of speech, again to the amusement of the others.

I returned to my position without a word, somewhat hurriedly this time. He was all smiles now, and extremely deferential.

"Ready?" he asked after a lengthy pause.

I nodded. Even then, he waited another second or two, like a pitcher tantalizing an impatient hitter by repeatedly shaking off his catcher's signs. And when Lester finally served, his ferocity was suddenly replaced by a softly hit pooper that barely arrived into the service box, and I returned it so poorly, he promptly put it away for still another point, again to the amusement of all.

The match seesawed to 13-all, growing sloppier as it progressed, each of us scoring on the other's errors. Point after point slipped away from me as I failed to execute ordinarily simple shots. I felt as though I were losing control of my feet, twice stumbling over myself, once so foolishly, I checked to see if a shoelace had come untied. This sudden gracelessness made me twice as ineffective as my awkward opponent, who had never known how to be otherwise. Nor did he have to cheat again, for the threat alone kept me on edge.

It was 14-all when I won back the service, prepared to win the final two points at long last. It had been a tedious and frustrating comedy of errors, and I wanted to be done with it. To those who claim that competition brings out the worst in people, this game was the ultimate illustration. No doubt I would win but I would taste no pride in victory.

I served, Stillson returned, and the volleying began—but only briefly, for Stillson had no intention of letting me dominate the point. As I was about to pivot into what should be the putaway shot, I found my foot glued to the floor—with his foot firmly planted on it. Immobilized, I could make no swing, and Lester immediately claimed the point.

This time, I would not permit it. "Lester," I tried to smile, "you were hard on my foot."

"I was what?"

"We'll call it a 'let'," I said. "Replay the point."

"Go to hell. You lost it. Period." And he scooped up the ball to gain possession which, the way he viewed it, brought him nine-tenths of the right to the service box.

"I must disagree," I said, standing my ground in that same sacred area.

He was not two feet from me, staring at me as though I were insane. Then he turned to the gallery and the dozen or more spectators, his manner projecting a long-suffering patience that was now bringing him to the end of his rope.

"Gentlemen," he called out, "Littlefield claims a 'let'. I don't know why, but if any of you saw a reason for it, let's hear it."

"Play the game!" someone cried out.

"Yeah. Serve 'em up, Lester."

Their laughter was strident, unquestionably very much in his camp. Had no one seen that foot on mine? Why were they rooting so hard for him? Could anyone really imagine Lester Stillson ever being an *underdog*? Then it occurred to me that there was little difference between the way this game was being played and the way all these men ran their businesses. What Lester was doing did not shock them. They saw only what they chose to see, accepting cheating and deceit; it mattered little to them as long as there was profit or, in this case, entertainment.

Lester laughed. Having practically won his victory, he pulled the biggest surprise of all and loudly reversed himself.

"Look, if you're so damn sure it's a 'let', okay, let's call it a 'let'," and with an exquisite gall only Lester could muster, he added, "I don't want to win *that* badly."

With that, he handed me the ball and walked to the receiver's box, gesturing to the gallery like a bruised martyr for which he received a healthy clatter of applause.

I was really quite debilitated. All desire seemed to ooze out of me like air from a punctured tire. It was the unanimity of the response that hurt, I suppose. For all my deference in the face of his violation of protocol, not one in the dozen appeared to support me. And when I prepared to serve again, the sharp edge of desire was dulled by the rocks of Lester's attrition. The slash of my racket lacked a proper authority, and he pounced on my service with a free-swinging recklessness as though he'd been withholding such shots for these last key points. I managed to get my racket on it, but the point was quickly his.

At 15–14, it was his service, and it suddenly crossed my mind that he might very well win, a prospect that made me boil. I quickly readied myself, but he was adjusting his shirt, tucking it under his shorts like one who could not possibly play on without being perfectly clothed.

"Oh, come on, Stillson," I mumbled.

"What's the penalty this time?"

"Old age, senility, perhaps even death," I quipped.

"You know something, Littlefield? You're not much of a gentleman at all."

"Oh, for Christ's sake, serve it up, will you!"

Having sufficiently riled me, he obliged by serving, another languid change of pace, and this time I was careful to time in properly. I hit it firmly, high and away from him, but he handled it deftly off the rear wall. I moved in to put it away, attempting a passing shot along the right wall, trapping Lester behind me. He raced to the rear wall again with a remarkable burst of speed from those bandy little legs, making a surprisingly agile return. Indeed, I was so amazed, I was a half-step late in recovering, just managing to tap it into the left corner. I was then doubly amazed to see him dashing back to the front court with the speed and stamina of an untiring youth, then snapping his racket at the ball with fresh power, and I knew at once there was no way I could return it.

The game was over.

Immediately, the gallery erupted. One would think Bobby Riggs had just outpunched Muhammed Ali. In less than a few seconds, they were down the stairs, exploding onto the court like Met fans after the playoffs. They lifted him to their shoulders and carried him through the halls in blustering admiration.

"Champagne!" he cried out when they reached the locker room. "Where's the champagne!" And he sent the attendant to get as many bottles as they could find, iced, uniced, it mattered not. When they returned with three, Stillson himself uncorked one, roaring with laughter, and poured the first drink over his own sweaty head.

"How do you like that!" he laughed. "Champagne baths two days in a row!"

Then he handed the bottle to me, the generosity of the victor.

I could barely tolerate the sight of it, but I should have known how rejection would be interpreted by such a man.

"You know something, Littlefield? You're a cream puff. Guys like you, you don't know how to win. You've had life so easy, you think the world will roll over every time you show your pretty face."

I concentrated on getting out of my jock, pretending all this was related to someone else, foolishly assuming that my indifference would silence him. Instead, he came at me with renewed vigor.

"Shit, you can't even look a man in the eye, Littlefield. I'll bet you never had to fight for anything in your life. It's all there in your goddam books. Huh, those books! I don't believe a minute of them. They're all fake, just like you're a fake. There ain't a real thing in them, all that bullshit about how you 'tested your mettle.' What fucking drivel!"

He punctuated his diatribe with a laugh and another slug of champagne, then laughed again as he withdrew the bottle. He had them, all right. Quite obviously, it pleased them to agree with him, if only for the moment. Even the attorney whose firm was connected with my publisher—he, too, was laughing.

This was not a role to which I was accustomed—the innocent bearing the brunt of inequities projected by the powerful. I remembered a cynical quote, "The reward for virtue is more punishment," which I had once found amusing, but now my head was being pounded by a different drumming. There would be repercussions. Mountains would surely be made of this affair. The columns would have a party with it, twisting the account to suit their needs. A stupid game of squash, the fulminations of a cheater, the humiliating awareness of myself standing there numbly, scratching my buttocks for want of an action, wanting to turn away yet too humiliated even to do that while his words echoed through my head in an eerie audible instant replay, the sort of device used in old movies to suggest an oncoming madness.

It wasn't until I moved into the shower room that I began to rally with a spasm of rage, a rage that coursed through me with such incredible speed, my body shook like an automobile engine suddenly revved up beyond its capacity. Humiliation dissolved in the exhilaration of my anger.

I hated that man. I don't believe I'd ever hated anyone before. The sense of it so overwhelmed me, I had trouble handling it. My entire being felt strange, as if possessed by an alien force. An incredible new power surged through me. My chest seemed to expand to herculean proportions. I felt I could ram my fist through the wall. In a strange way, the experience became enormously satisfying, as if this were the real purpose of the incident, a magnificent rejuvenation of my spirit that drummed against my ribs and almost made me weep with joy. In a fitting complement to this emotion, I reached for the shower knob and turned on a slashing icy spray and stood defiantly under it. I never even felt a chill, my entire body was under the control of my mind. At that moment, I could have walked barefooted over scorching coals.

Something was happening here. I could feel the depths of it. Some new insight into the very essence of what I was as a man. I had never been unkind and certainly not cruel. By dint of my affability, I had achieved inordinate success. Now, it seemed, an excruciating rage had been festering within me, too long crushed under a mass of gentlemanliness and chic sophistication. My debonair style had been, more than likely, an unwitting put-on to achieve popularity. The prince would turn out to be less charming than vengeful.

I exulted in my new-found anger. The pleasure of hating Lester seemed far in excess of whatever love I'd felt for anyone. A stirring, challenging sanguinity made me feel more intensely alive than I'd ever felt before. My head literally bubbled with grandiose prospects to satisfy my hunger for revenge. I even considered the thrill of killing him with my bare hands, then laughed at the fantasy. I was touched with madness and had never been happier.

So it was that the man who had liberated me, I now determined to destroy—a vicious little irony that was not lost on me. The name of the game was vengeance and I would learn to play it. I was, after all, a Littlefield, descendant of a rich lineage with a penchant for survival that could make Lester Stillson's biography seem pallid.

Preposterous situations cry out for preposterous solutions, and I spun the wheels for the right one. Then I heard the sound of his voice again, this time barking into a locker room telephone and, I gathered, the ear of his wife in her palatial boudoir: "No, dammit, I've got a meeting . . . Yes, another meeting . . . Wait up, don't wait up, I couldn't care less . . . ," whereupon he slammed the receiver to its cradle as though it were a fist in her face, then laughed with the macho arrogance of a teenager impressing his peers. "The bitch must be in heat," he quipped in a glittering summation of a great marriage.

Immediately, there it was. My bright quicksilver mind took hold with my new Machiavellian drive. Here, I saw, was a piece of fruit ripe for the plucking.

By God, I would put the horns of the cuckold on his evil head!

4

Let it be known that Patricia Clark Stillson was no ordinary housewife. To begin with, she was an heiress with a link to U.S. Steel worth an estimated $60,000,000. Having met her once or twice at charity affairs, I also knew she was extremely attractive, a factor that seemed relevant enough at the moment. She was a slender, leggy lady approximately my age with a gracious manner that always led to speculations on what such a woman was doing with the likes of Lester. A lion and a ewe sort of union. But, then, who could ever explain what forces brought people together.

Let it also be known that sexual liaisons with married women had never been my cup of tea. However often I had been tempted in my lengthy bachelor's career, I had scrupulously demurred, sometimes in the face of extremely appetizing arrangements. Besides, there were always enough unmarried ladies to bed down with.

This confrontation, then, was a significant first for me, especially as the opening gambit of my new aggressiveness. I had called her that afternoon on the pretext of soliciting support for a literary magazine I'd been associated with and found myself amused at the ease with which I slid into conmanship.

"Why, of course," Patricia replied. She didn't even seem surprised. "Why don't you come over this evening for a drink?"

Arriving at the Stillson mansion, just off Fifth Avenue in the low seventies, I rang the bell with the confidence of a bank robber holding the combination to the safe. It was Patricia who answered the door, not a servant, delighting me with a warm smile and casual attire.

Her hand was warm as she led me inside, a home as elegant as the lady was casual. Spacious rooms fanned out before me, a broad spiral staircase, antique brick fireplace, original oils by Matisse, Léger, Levine, sculpture by Dubuffet, sketches by Picasso. As I followed her through these sumptuous rooms en route to the bar, we were pursued by a Schubert quartet filtering through hidden speakers, just loud enough to hear if one cared to listen. It was all so tasteful, one wondered where Lester lived. Even his portrait, gold-framed over the living room mantel, was a romantic study of a pensive man, legs crossed as he sat in a dark velvet-covered chair, his manner so civilized and sensitive, my stomach knotted in contempt for the whoredom of the painter.

She must have seen the telltale tightening of my jaw.

"You know my husband, of course."

"Slightly," I worked for a smile.

"Is that possible?"

We sat, and I rattled the cubes in my drink, raising the glass for a toast. "Congratulations on the championship, Patricia."

"Oh, that . . . well, I suppose it's preferable to win than to lose."

"There are some who say it's the *only* thing."

She replied with a soft sigh and an ever-so-slight shaking of her head. "Football is played by boring overgrown children and watched by boring underdeveloped adults."

"What about your husband?"

She shrugged. "A form of masturbation."

"I'll drink to that," I said.

"To masturbation, then," she raised her glass, and we sipped to a background of muted strings.

It was so ludicrous, I had to laugh out loud.

"Well . . . I consider this a rare compliment, Gordon; you never so much as smile on television."

"Is that a fact?" I truly wondered.

She had an endearing way of shrugging, her left shoulder and ear gently edging toward each other. "You *are* dour, you know. You always look as if you'd just caught a whiff of something terribly noxious." Then, conciliatory: "Perhaps we should get our television adjusted."

I stared at her, stripping that pale blue blouse in my mind's eye, cupping her breast in my demanding hand, sinking my teeth in the graceful neck. Was it not extremely important to leave one's mark for the cuckolded victim? I could feel a tentative stirring in my crotch, and I thought, well why not, it was my birthday, wasn't it?

"You wanted to discuss some literary project? . . ." she asked.

"No . . . not really." I said. It just slipped out that way, the first move toward Armageddon.

"Oh?"

She had a remarkable capacity to make a brilliant summation with a simple word. That "oh" laid a spotlight on the spectacle I was making of myself. I did not have the slightest notion of what to say next, sensing only a vague fear of dissembling. The thought of such a submission riled me to the quick. I did not come here to supplicate. Quite the contrary, it was the new tiger in me that was setting the styles. Nor was I about to play coy games with this lady in one of those suave, devious seductions à la David Niven, say. This was going to be Errol Flynn or bust. Valiantly, then, I squared my shoulders and threw down the gauntlet.

"Actually, I came here to seduce you," I said, then blanched at the sound of my own words. I would have pulled them back if I could, or at least redelivered them with a whimsical provocative twinkle in my eye. But I had been so brash and insulting, I sat rigidly on guard lest she suddenly throw her drink, or an ash tray, at me.

Instead, she smiled, canting her head to indicate curiosity. "How fascinating! I haven't been propositioned in years." She made it sound as though I had challenged her to a Scrabble game.

"I'm serious, Patricia."

"Please, call me Pat. As long as we've become intimate . . ."

"Thank you, Pat."

Pause.

"Well, what am I supposed to do?" she asked. "Do I take you upstairs, or strip for you here? Can't we talk to each other first?"

"Certainly . . . I wouldn't think of ——"

"I mean, you'll have to excuse me, Gordon. I feel so inexperienced——"

"Of course."

"Do you do this sort of thing often?"

"No . . . as a matter of fact—"

"Then, it *is* flattering, isn't it. I'm very flattered, you know."

Curiously, she was enjoying this far more than I. In fact, I found myself about to be boiled in scented oil. The time had come to change the pattern. I wasn't even a D. Niven at this stage, much less an E. Flynn. The entire affair was moving from drama to farce. I speculated on crossing to the sofa where she sat and making an outright pass. A frontal attack, as it were. That I restrained myself was due less to manners than discretion. What then? I asked myself, my mind groping blindly in an oncoming fog. It was to my credit, then, that my solution would be the honest one. I would tell her the truth. I would disarm her with the *whole* truth, this time. A confessional, as it were, replete with doleful pathos and neurotic vulnerability. Not Niven or Flynn, then, but M. Brando.

"Pat, let me explain . . . I'm all twisted about this," I stammered. "The real reason is, well, I despise your husband." Then, generating the proper gall, I flashed my verbal phallus: "What I mean is, I came here to cuckold him."

This time, she really laughed.

Apparently, it was one of those scenes wherein everything I said would be taken as a joke. She simply could not believe I was in earnest. Strangely enough, I could understand this and could see the joke from where she sat. Unfortunately, however, I did not know how to rectify it. I was beginning to suspect that this entire episode was turning into a colossal defeat.

What was left for me now but to tell it all, the whole story from the squash game to the locker room diatribe, even my cold shower zest for retribution. She listened, intrigued at last by my ardor. Indeed, the way I told it, one would think her husband had actually stabbed me in the back. As a result, she did not laugh this time. In fact, she was all sympathy.

"I know . . . he simply must win. It's a form of breathing for him. If he didn't win, he'd suffocate."

It was a breakthrough, all right. The joke was over, and her mouth turned its lines from amusement to acrimony as though she had switched those classic masks of drama. She despised him, after all. At least we now had something in common.

"It's never enough for him to win; he has to humiliate

his victims," and she vehemently mashed her cigarette in the ashtray. "He used to tell me he loved me. Every night, as a matter of fact. I liked that. Then I discovered he was screwing my maid."

I had to wonder why she permitted such a marriage to continue, but said nothing, having long since decided that such mysteries were rarely worth pursuing.

She sighed, shook her head, commiserating with her own past.

"Curious . . . how I found a man like him so appealing. I guess it was because he *did* things. I was sick of the men who didn't have to."

The classic story of the idle rich going slumming and loving the change. She went on about that, how Lester's poor-boy background in New York made him seem romantic, how his street-tough aggressive manner excited her. Lester had become successful enough, to be sure. An extremely well paid lawyer with his show business clientele. He was known as a resourceful in-fighter who manipulated lucrative deals—then took substantial cuts of the take. An agent more than a lawyer, one might say. Lester had the gift of making his most celebrated clients seem dependent upon him, as though *he* were the talented one and the star merely his instrument. He used everyone to promote himself—precisely the reverse of the usual relationship. He was smart, all right, for everyone was intrigued by the world of motion pictures and Lester was known as a gold mine of intimate gossip.

Just as curiously, I understood the attraction, for I knew a number of her usual dilettantish suitors, scions of in-bred Eastern moneyed families with stylish tastes in the arts and politics but very little hunger for life. I could also picture an ambitious interloper like Lester abrasively weaving among them, finding the weakness of his rivals while exposing the veneer of his own strength.

"He was quite amazing," she went on. "I mean, when

he courted, he never let me forget him. Wherever I went, Newport, Palm Beach, Rome, once even in Istanbul, he would send me a 'treat': a box of frozen Milky Ways, would you believe it? A link to *his* childhood. I laughed at the whole affair, but it didn't stop him. Nothing stopped him. 'You don't belong with those people!' he would say, and I would wonder what it would be like to go with a man like him."

She blushed at the thought, then smiled to confess her embarrassment. "He was such a little tiger, I found myself sexually attracted to him."

I recalled the gossip about their marriage six or seven years ago, then the news a few years after when he bought the last-place Bulls for $18,000,000 (of her money). Neither the marriage nor the world of professional football would ever be the same again.

"The Bulls . . ." she mused. "Bull, bull-oney, bullshit. I used to dream about bulls, would you believe it? Big bull cocks as long as your arm. Bulls bullshitting all over my room. Everywhere I went there were bulls." She spoke with a trace of hysteria rising in her voice. I did not have the slightest notion of where she was heading. "He has this stupid toy to play with. It's all that matters to him, that toy. Take it away and he'd probably go mad."

A clock was chiming in some nearby parlor, a soft melodic concatenation that interspersed with Mozart strings, and I could not help but wonder how close I was to the end of my birthday.

"He is obsessed with the Bulls, you know? When the football season begins, he is driven by demons. There is nothing else. Nothing. And if he wins the Superbowl . . ." She winced at her own thoughts, as if the consequences of the victory would be too horrendous to cope with.

If he wins the Superbowl? There seemed but small question of it. Lester Stillson will win the Superbowl, and he will ride through this city like an emperor. Everyone will accept his politics, his morality, his brand of toothpaste, his insidious moustache. His grandeur will multiply like poisonous mushrooms after a three-day rain. Everything he ever did will be justified, every lie, every betrayal, every dead body that lay in his wake.

What followed in my head, then, was a phenomenon I would never be able to reconstruct exactly. The old cartoon has the light bulb flashing inside one's head. Creative people have the ecstasy of it every so often, the artist's brush that takes an unpremeditated turn revealing a majestic insight into beauty; the composer rambles over the keyboard and his fingers combine to strike a chord that fills the room with exquisite sound. For me, on that sofa, staring at the painting, it was simply an idea fathered by hate and mothered by boredom. I let it leak out slowly, delicately, savoring every word as my mind worked to adjust.

"My dear Patricia," I said. "He really doesn't have to win when you get right down to it."

So simple, yet so frightening. The thought was so extraordinary, it could not but open the floodgates, and a million invisible fairies began dancing inside my skin. It was the sheer boldness of the idea that loomed so awesomely. How could I ever consider it, much less know for a certainty that yes, I would do it, come hell or high water! Nor was I oblivious to the complexity of its implementation, even at that preposterous moment. If I was biting off a truly gargantuan hunk, not for a moment did I doubt the sharpness of my teeth.

She must have sensed what they call vibrations, for she looked at me strangely.

"He doesn't?" she asked.

"I'm thinking . . ."

"Well, kindly think out loud."

I wasn't sure I was ready. It was as if I were plotting

Lester's assassination. How had I gotten to this point? I had come for cuckoldry, not to make history. Yet the more I played with it, the more reasonable it became. It was magnificent stuff, all right. The deft manipulation of caprice. I found myself driven forward by some compelling force from which I could not restrain myself.

"I'm thinking that a man such as your husband lends himself to the vengeance of his enemies. . . ."

"He does, he does," she said with impatience.

"I can picture any number of them who share such an emotion."

"A number of Bulls, no doubt?"

"No doubt," I agreed.

"Fine. How much would it cost?" she asked.

"If you have to ask, you can't afford it," I said.

"I withdraw the question, then."

"A hundred thousand dollars," I said.

She snapped her fingers to suggest its simplicity.

"No check, my dear. One hundred dollar bills only," I advised.

"Goodness, just like Watergate."

"Vengeance makes plumbers of us all."

"And if we get caught, whom do *we* blame it on?"

"The trick is *not* to get caught. *No* one must know."

"Not even the players?"

"You're teasing me, Pat."

She shrugged in that endearing way of hers.

"And suppose they win?" she asked.

"If you'll pardon the colloquialism, no way."

"My dear Gordon, you underrate my husband."

"Only the Almighty could win with this handicap."

"Gordon . . ." she sighed in warning.

"Even if Lester has Him in his pocket, *no way.*"

That determined, my mind segued into new ideas. Patricia, however, had ideas of her own.

"Well, I'm ready, Gordon."

"Ready?"

"Certainly. Let's make love."

I admit to being perplexed by this attack on my initiative. I had come for revenge, not to service her. The entire scene had blown my mind, as they say, and I needed time to adjust. But she had made more compelling adjustments, it seemed. She set her tall glass on the marble table in front of us and moved directly to my side on the huge davenport. Before I could react, a hand rested warmly on mine, another began caressing the back of my neck, and when I turned to look at her, her lips appeared out of nowhere. The die was cast. Her arms reached around me with a burst of passion, and her teeth rammed into mine, her tongue probing my inner lips like a silver teaspoon scooping out the clinging remains of a chocolate mousse. Her hand went burrowing under my jacket, into buttons and buttonholes, fingernails knifing erotically into ribs, working lower and lower to my belt line, never missing a button or buckle or clasp, however small or hidden. Even my zipper, not at all obliging to me, seemed to slide on grease at her touch. My head was scheming in the clouds, alive with the most scintillating prospects I'd ever dared to face, while my genitals were in her hand, flipping in futility this way and that, in a variety of her demanding manipulations. If I may paraphrase the great Yogi Berra, how could I think and screw at the same time?

Of course, *this* was what she was serious about. The fix was just conversation to her, or so I immediately suspected, while my own head could deal with nothing else. Indeed, I could hardly feel her hand as it cradled, stroked, fondled, and squeezed. She was still kissing me, beginning again at my neck not two inches behind my ear, then tracing a seductive route down my chest to my stomach, alternately licking and nipping at flesh wherever it was free of the bone, while that warm hand kept working on my cock, a probing thumb teasing the aperture, a pair of fingernails edging along the sensitive undersurface.

Then I chanced to look up at that portrait again, and the blood rushed to my instantly swelling organ. The impact was truly inspirational. By God, I would take both his wife *and* his team!

This erotic response so gratified her very soul, her lips left my navel and gradually encircled my erect tool. My eyes lingered on Lester's face, prepared to sneer like a vindictive schoolboy at this moment of triumph, but the view was blocked by a muff of her hair, the tantalizing crotch-V canted on its side not three inches in front of my lips. I reached out to surround her buttocks, pulling her to me until I was burrowing my tongue past the palpitating labia. Thus we lay, indulging ourselves with mindless abandon while a sordid chapter in the history of sport had to wait. She was magnificent, both as seducer and seducee, far more responsive now because of our intimacy, occasionally retreating from her tonguing to register an ecstatic, breathtaking sigh. My own throbbing readiness was a tinderbox of such fresh desire, I could no longer wait for the consummating action that would surely take us both to Nirvana.

As if on cue, we abandoned the *soixante-neuf*, rearranging our bodies on and off the davenport for a proper coitus, but not without sacrificing my own need to face that portrait in the process. Indeed, I who was about to mount the wife turned for one final glance at the husband that I might debauch that phony serenity, only to see the beady eyes suddenly leering, the mouth twisted in a lascivious grin.

It was Lester Stillson, the intruder, in the flesh.

"Go right ahead," he said, catching my querulous eye. "Please . . . I'd like to see how you handle her." And he sat down across from us for a front-row view of it.

My God, here was cuckoldry in the raw. He was taunting me with a classic ploy of the ultra-arrogant man. The answer was to ram it into her with appropriate fanfare, then watch him disintegrate, and I conjured up triumphant images of my own gloating smile as we raced toward a climax embellished with tantalizing cries and ecstatic moans.

What's more, Patricia seemed indifferent to his presence, or, perhaps, inspired by it, for she tugged at my cock while her legs spread to welcome me. I let loose a cry of anticipation and moved to complete the coupling.

But even as I did, I felt the sap draining from me. My body was losing that marvelous dramatic tension that precedes sex, my mind shifting treacherously to an awareness of oncoming failure. The blood that had rushed so eloquently to fill my phallus now found cause to retreat, seeping out of those myriad capillaries as though beckoned by some insidious power I could not withstand. Indeed, I had not even entered her when the damned thing went limp in her hand.

She sighed in despair, then fell back on the davenport to suffer the pangs of unrequited sex.

Lester, of course, could not resist gloating. "You Princeton men . . . you can't even shit if the door is open."

What could I say? I rolled away from her, rallying whatever poise I could under such humiliating circumstances, all too aware of the frequency with which this man had done me in. I busied my hands with my clothing while my mind worked hard at the possibilities. How could one turn this defeat into a victory?

It was Pat who went into action.

"I think you ought to apologize to Gordon, dear," she began, sounding more like a parent castigating a child. "I thought your nastiness at the gym was inexcusable."

I could only imagine the litany of grievances he had yet to redress her for.

"You're a lot smarter than I thought," he said to me.

"Let's just say I learn quickly," I replied, shooting for modesty.

The truth was, I suddenly *did* realize what was happening. I had totally misread my power. Or, more accurately, the lack of his. Cuckoldry, it seemed, had its own ethos. To wit, it was not I, the perpetrator, who was the vulnerable one, but Lester, the victim (or, in this case, the *near* victim) whose status was at bay. In the end, it was he who would be the supplicant, eager for the affair to be silenced. *His* reputation was at stake, not mine. The owner of the Bulls, no less. Not the Cardinals, or the Saints, or the gentle Dolphins. But the *Bulls.* The symbolisms were so marvelous, I could barely contain my amusement.

Lester saw all the nuances, of course. He must have spent the moment hating her almost as much as he enjoyed humiliating me. He regarded her with the barest of an icy glance, then turned to me, raising his glass in a gesture that I took to confirm her wishes.

"I suppose you want four seats on the fifty for next season, eh?" And even before I could reply: "Okay, you got 'em."

"That's very kind of you, Lester," I replied, "but no thanks."

He shrugged, having volunteered his bit. I was not so easy to dispose of, however, for I had far grander fish to fry. That golden glow still lit up my brain, sending endless shots of energy through me. Here was my big chance. If I were going to implement my idea, this was definitely the time to start the wheels a-rolling.

"I was thinking, Lester . . . I might enjoy doing a book about your club. 'Ten Days to the Superbowl,' that sort of thing. From the inside, of course."

"What!"

"I'd like to go to work for your organization, as part of your equipment crew, perhaps. One of those chaps who run out on the field with the Gatorade during time-outs. I'd get a fine book out of it."

He was wary, obviously confused. I could see him thrashing it around.

"Perhaps I was wrong about the club, Lester," I persisted. "I mean, if they're as great as you believe, I'll see it and write it. Besides, you get an unpaid employee." Then, to cement the plan: "Lester, this is my forte. I once waited on tables at a White House dinner. Remember that article? Another time I played a small part in a hardcore porno film. The intimacy feeds my imagination. The literary potential is there, without question. And, I might add, much favorable attention to your organization."

And, I might also add, a marvelous cover for my hanky-panky.

All this was greeted with silence, no doubt inspired by skepticism. Well, I could not fault him for that. The easiest thing in the world would be to say no.

"You gotta be out of your fucking mind!" he said.

5

Arriving home, I was somewhat surprised to note that it was still my birthday. I poured myself a nightcap, kicked off my shoes, and reclined in my chair to contemplate what had been a most incredible day. From this vantage point in time and weariness, the day had had a phantasmagorical cast to it, a series of weird transitions so alien to me, I could hardly begin to absorb them.

To bet $1000 on a squash game?
To cuckold Lester Stillson?
To fix the Superbowl?

I really had to laugh at such preposterous aberrations. It all seemed like a joke I must have been playing on myself for which I could not possibly be held responsible. A day of madness to liberate the troubled spirit, as it were. One recognizes the scenario: I would enjoy the memory. I might even recount it to a few friends one day, but that would be all. It was a matter to be dismissed. There would be no more of the unforgettable Lester and his appealing wife—and all those Stillson House horrors. No doubt we would all forgive and forget, if for no other reason than it was to everyone's advantage to do so.

So I languished the last eight minutes to midnight, watching the slowly shifting digits of my clock as I prepared to retire the day with my somewhat battered psyche. Surely, everything would be peaceful in the morning.

It was. The long night's sleep was a dreamless pleasure, and it was well into the day before I was awakened by the ringing telephone.

"Hello?"

"My dear Gordon, good morning, good morning . . ."

I had no trouble recognizing the soft, throaty voice of Patricia Stillson.

"Well, how are you, Patricia?"

"Pat," she corrected me.

"Sorry, Pat."

"I've no desire for small talk. I've a sack of groceries here and I wanted to be certain you were home."

"Groceries?"

"I'm delivering immediately."

And the phone, as my Irish friends might say, went as dead as Kelsey's nuts. She must have had a taxi waiting, for I was just finishing my ablutions when she arrived.

She smiled, amused by the look of me. She was as elegantly beautiful as she'd been casual the day before. Wrapped in a magnificent mink (her day coat, I supposed) with matching hat, her lovely face radiant with tasteful make-up and exposure of winter chill. She came in with a large loaded shopping bag.

I ushered her inside where she set the sack on my dining room table, then tossed her mink to a chair. I stood by as she pulled out a huge cereal box, paper towels, family-sized loaves of bread, a few apples. Then she reached the bottom, extracted a beautiful wooden cigar box on which

I noted the celebrated Upmann label. Havana cigars. Fifty of the finest, and I smiled with anticipation. A birthday gift, I mused. Ceremoniously, she set it on the table, quickly returning all other items to the sack.

"Well, open it," she said.

I pried open the slender nailed lid, prepared to extend my appreciation at the first aromatic whiff.

Not cigars, as it turned out, but a box full of neatly packaged $100 bills.

I gasped.

"My, how everything surprises you," she quipped, obviously surprised at me. "What's the matter with you anyway?"

There were dozens of thick packets, beautifully beribboned in keeping with the holiday season. She had even sprinkled them with spray-on gold dust to add to the glitter.

I had never seen so much money and I was forced to say so. The sight was overwhelming, even to a man of means.

"It's quite dazzling, I daresay . . ."

She helped herself to an apple, bit audibly into its juicy pulp.

"It's real, I assure you, Gordon. Unmarked, unrecorded, unknown. I mean that. Nobody knows I have it. Nobody knows I'm giving it to you. What's more, there's no way to check it. One hundred thousand, just as you asked." Then she smiled.

"I hope you're satisfied," she added.

Mostly, I was perplexed.

"As I recall, Pat, old Lester *rejected* my offer."

"You underestimate me," she twinkled, then broke into a smile that might have made the devil jealous. "Gordon . . . we're in business!"

It was altogether a startling piece of news, so sudden I could be excused my doubts. For all the apparent perfection of its parts, there was something unseemly about the project now. Was it because I had so recently abandoned it? Or because she had reversed that all by herself? What's more, she had implemented it, dumping it in my lap all sprinkled with gold dust. How could I not rebel? Was this the proper opening for so enterprising a scheme, especially in light of my regenerative rage that had inspired it? Unlike Lester, I was not a man to feed off the power and wealth of such a woman, certainly not when I'd been looking for an ultimate challenge to my own ennui.

"Well, well . . . ," she said, obviously appalled at my lack of enthusiasm. "What do we have here, a man or a mouse?" completely missing the point. After all, was she not throwing a glittering piece of cheese at me in order to turn me into a mouse? Nor did I appreciate still another challenge to my manhood, certainly not from Lester Stillson's wife. I would deal with my own, thank you, when and how I saw fit.

She took another bite of the apple, tossed it into the sack. Then she returned to the cash, started to put it all back in the cigar box like an unsuccessful salesman putting away his wares.

I must admit, she got to me. When one considers it, the whole thing was an amazing visual experience. My eyes feasted on those neat, crisp, sparkling piles of money and the absolutely beautiful woman who was handling them. It was all for me, for the taking, as they say. The sight alone was so bewitching, how could I resist it? One does not debate such matters, one leaps at them.

I leaped. I grabbed her wrist with one hand, scooped up the cigar box with the other, then pulled her away from the table and into the bedroom. She protested as I knew she would. "No, Gordon. . . . Stop, you're hurting me. . . ." The sort of thing that no sensible rapist pays attention to. And I was going to rape her, I admitted that to myself. I might have tried to seduce her, but that was not the way I wanted it to be. In fact, her cries excited me. I even provoked them by twisting her arm, and when we reached my bed, I literally threw her onto it, spilled the cigar box of cash all over her, then pounced into action.

The whole point was, I wanted to cement the fix by taking her on the money itself.

She was frightened, all right, crying out "No, Gordon . . . No . . . No . . . No!" loudly enough for the neighbors, but it mattered not. I ripped off her blouse, then her bra, and buried my head in her breasts, my lips on one, my hand on the other. Inside my pants, my erection achieved steellike rigidity as I straddled her body, opening my belt to unzip. We were clothes restricted as I manipulated her, so hungry was I for release, but that, too, didn't matter— in fact, it enhanced the erotic sense of it. My knees pried her legs apart, forced an entrance. More cries, more resistance. Whatever, she could enjoy it or not, I was unconcerned for such niceties. I began to work majestically inside her, protesting her dry resistance. My hands clasped her lower back, just above the buttocks, forcing a vicelike meld of our bodies as I drove in circles, swivel hipped. My teeth found her breasts, biting, this time, to leave a mark for Lester to take note of. Look, I commanded, look at who was here, you miserable bastard! But even as I contemplated so great a triumph, I sensed he would never notice, I was biting in vain. Indeed, the whole affair seemed in vain for there was simply no response. A noncohabital coitus. For the first time in my lover's life, I felt I might as well be delving into the dead.

"Fuck you, Lester Stillson!" I cried out in rage.

And suddenly, it changed everything.

"Oh my God!" she sighed, and began to move under me. There was heat in her flesh, a hand went digging in my shoulder and tugged at my hair as if it were the last life-saving shrub on the edge of a cliff. With a burst of ferocity, her mouth joined mine, digging her teeth into my lips until I cried out in pain. Her legs enveloped me, heels digging into calves, and she began to writhe and twist with an incredible burst of strength, snapping her body as she flipped me from side to side, arching her back under me with the power of a wrestler, up and down, this way and that. Her nails raked my shoulders like moving barbed wire, another hand beat against my back in rhythm with her thrusts, and I would have sworn still another hand kept tugging at the hair behind my head. Her passion was overwhelming, I had never known anything quite like it. And when she approached orgasm, she drew on a fantastic reserve of speed and stamina, emitting a wail that topped a police siren, and I found myself ejaculating with such intensity, I thought I would never be able to copulate again.

We fell back spent, sucking in air like a skin diver after a four-minute submersion. I rolled over, incredulous, my testes feeling as though they'd been shot off. I could barely touch myself, so sensitive were my nerve endings. When I finally turned my head, I saw her staring into space, no longer solemn but on the brink of laughter.

"What's so funny?" I asked.

"I always laugh when I come. What a way to get even!"

"Two great libidos with a single thought."

She laughed again. "Perhaps we've invented a new kind of sex therapy."

My head was cradled in her arm, and she turned her face to nuzzle my ear. It was so endearing, I didn't want it to end. But it did—with the last thing I wanted to face: a tenuous question of morality.

"Tell me honestly," she began, her voice as fragile as a troubled schoolgirl's. "Isn't this Superbowl business of ours a rather terrible thing?"

"The fix?"

She winced at the word, then nodded.

It was a stopper, all right. Illicit sex has a way of disturbing the conscience.

"Depends on your point of view," I said.

"Well, what's yours?"

It was a moment of real crisis, demanding the best of me. Having expended my libido, I rallied my intellect. It was gratifying to hear the words roll easily off my tongue.

"A terrible thing, as you put it, is to do harm to innocents. But we're dealing with a football game where it's merely a question of who wins and who loses, a matter of absolutely *no* consequence. You'll see how ridiculous the whole affair is, a colossal hype, Pat, run by and for ad men, TV promoters, wheeler-dealers, all those flaks making a big thing out of nothing, while the public is told it's the greatest thing since the Declaration of Independence!"

I stopped to catch my breath, pleased that she was listening to me as though it were gospel.

"Then there's Lester," I went on. "He sits in the middle of it, his greedy arms reaching out in all directions like a hungry octopus, manipulating people to satisfy his ego, making up his own rules in a way that turns professional sports into a travesty. What are we doing if not thwarting all that evil nonsense? A service to Lester's victims, I daresay. And as for all the other Superbowlers—the mass of so-called fans that make up this country of ours—it's like taking candy from a baby who's been eating too much candy in the first place!"

I finished with my hands raised high above the bed like a minister blessing his flock.

"Amen," she said, then reached out to me again, renewing a crush of kisses that revived our hunger for each other.

"You're really too much for me, Gordon," she whispered.

It was a final source of satisfaction.

6

The fix itself was the largest puzzlement of all. No one had yet written the guide book on how to fix the Superbowl. How to get into gear? When tackling any new work, I'd learned to expect a number of false starts however much I tried to avoid them. My own rule of thumb as a writer had always been to plunge in and, if necessary, suffer the consequences, hoping for progress in the trial-and-error procedure. All too often, writers tend to labor over their work, so intent on perfection they cannot see the forest for the trees. DON'T DO IT PERFECTLY, JUST DO IT! read a sign over my desk, a warning against all those unrealistic demands I might make on myself.

In this matter, however, I was facing a whole other ballgame. One doesn't plunge into this one, one slides in under the door. It was going to be all trial and *no* error, no rewrites permitted, one wrong turn and I'd be sinking in quicksand.

Almost sixty years ago, a young Chicago boy pleaded with the great Shoeless Joe Jackson "Say it ain't so, Joe" as the ballplayer emerged from the Illinois Grand Jury

Room after confessing to the fixing of the 1919 World Series. "Yes, son, I'm afraid it is," Jackson had replied. That one of the greatest hitters of the time had actually been willing to sell out for $5000 and a bag of empty promises was the key. That seven others of the Chicago White Sox were with him, all essentially honest and dedicated men, reaffirms its impact. The Black Sox Scandal was of a different era, but there were significant similarities with the present to pique my interest. The 1919 club owner was the penurious Charles Comiskey, whose hunger for profits was at least as great as his hunger for the championship. Comiskey had broken promises to them all, infuriated them with petty irritants, and perhaps above all, refused to treat them with respect.

The point was obvious enough: Lester Stillson was an exaggerated version of a modern Comiskey. Clearly, there had to be at least as many malcontents and dissenters today. And did not the moral climate of the 1970s lend itself to cynical compromise even more than the immediate postwar year of 1919? One asks such a question then laughs at the obvious response: this was the generation of Vietnam, Watergate, of governmental lies and coverups, of colossal corporate swindling and exploitation, of assassination as government policy. Indeed, the fix seemed fitting; one could almost say that it *deserved* to be done as a logical derivative of our current mores. Had not our entire culture been inundated with the literature of decay? What were current films all about but the glorification of the psychopath? What was the incredible surge of pornography but the epitome of emptiness?

That I had not been able to resist the melancholia of becoming forty was at least partially related to these factors. I, who had grown up in an enlightened tradition of what was noble in man, had finally found myself overwhelmed by his lack of it.

I was not unaware of how such evaluations could be

criticized as self-serving. The road to hell is often paved with such lofty rationalizations, if I may amend an old saw. Yet it has also been written, When in Rome, do as the Romans do, and my Rome was spluttering in decline and hastening to its fall.

The scenario now called for action.

The fix, yes.

The concept was the thing. I had to forge an artful plan, its implementation requiring a very special finesse. I would definitely exclude the old Hollywood route wherein the wormy thug (Elisha Cook) threatens the star quarterback. Or even the more businesslike approach (Edward Arnold) and the sophisticated luncheon as prelude to a substantial bribe. That sort of thing was pure idiocy. I could not make a bigger mistake than to approach the quarterback, however great his alienation, not only because he made over $100,000 a year but because everything he did was in full view, duly noted by all. Even if he were a consummate artist at fakery, a poor quarterback performance tended to invite suspicion. By the same token, I would avoid the next great temptation: the running backs, even though a star halfback could stifle an offense without the slightest difficulty—and look good in the process. The very opposite approach was infinitely more artful. I would concentrate on less glamorous positions where a poor block, a sloppy tackle, a split-second delay on pass coverage might prove climactic. I would select two players, one on offense, one on defense, who seldom if ever handle the ball, relatively nameless and faceless, though vital to the totality of a team effort. The possibilities seemed limitless. An offensive tackle fails to keep a a charging defensive end from smothering the quarterback. A cornerback just misses a tackle on a third down sweep. An interior lineman induces a penalty by overeagerly moving on a crucial third down play to shatter the momentum of a scoring drive. Besides, what better place to find the true dissidents than among those on the lowest levels of the salary scale? Interior linemen do not drive Cadillacs, as they say. Black defensive backs are rarely seen on TV commercials.

If the 1919 World Series was a travesty of chaotic proportion, it was because poor organization made discovery almost inevitable. The problem had been rooted in the gamblers, a ratpack of greedy characters who dominated the fix with appalling callousness. Indeed, there had been open talk of the fix even before the opening game, so wildly were the odds shifting with the rumors. With hindsight, one could readily foresee the entire episode building to some inexorable tragedy. By the same token, I would organize the Superbowl to be very much the opposite. Here, except for two players unknown even to each other, no one would know. No gamblers would be involved in any way. I would be the sole manipulator, thereby protecting the integrity of the point spread, a completely exposure-proof set-up to inspire the total confidence of my charges, assuring them of maximal protection against discovery.

The big question, then, was Who? For the next twelve days, all my energies would have to be concentrated on that. If I were to pull this off, my success would be contingent upon those two choices.

7

My first confrontation with the New York Bulls proved comparable to an entrapment in a Dickensian madhouse. Uninhabited, even the locker room seemed eerie, each cubicle half alive with empty helmet, jersey, pants, shoes in living juxtaposition. From an adjacent room, a radio emitted static, having drifted between stations, sounding like a police car between calls. And when Sy Getz appeared, the melancholy equipment manager who was to be my mentor, he said nothing to me, not even a gesture to acknowledge my presence, but pushed a large laundry bin loaded with clean socks. I watched him as he examined them all, quickly tossing most of them into another bin, a few others to the floor.

"A hole—even a tiny one—can cause a blister," he snapped. "A blister hurts, gets favored, causes a pulled muscle. Pull a groin muscle and a player is out. Lose a player, lose a game. Lose a game, lose a championship. All because some jerk like you, maybe, didn't see the hole!" And, simulating a monumental fury, he raised a sock with his index finger sticking through the heel.

"I'm Gordon Littlefield," I said. "You must be Sy Getz."

"Wash your hands," he said, indicating I was to join him in Operation Hole Hunting. Obviously, he didn't want my germs infecting any blisters.

For all my diligence, I found no holes, though Sy did, sometimes after I'd passed them, at which time he would scowl at me as though I were a saboteur. I began probing those socks with exaggerated eagerness, fingers literally digging into the soft cotton, even to create my hole that I might raise a deficient sock in triumph. When I finally succeeded, he refused to look at me, bending lower into the bin so that I saw only his bald pate.

My second responsibility was more complex though hardly as crucial.

"That crate of footballs . . ." He pointed to the large table in the center of the locker room. "Open 'em up, take 'em out of the boxes, count 'em. There should be a dozen. You'll find marking pens in a cigar box. When the players come, they'll autograph 'em. See that they sign 'em all."

Then he paused for a moment, anticipating a question. I tried hard to think of one, but merely nodded politely. He seemed disappointed, even scowled, then disappeared into the back room.

Well, it was a proper assignment for me, the laying of pen on pigskin, and I waited for their arrival. There was always something significant about the first words the players would say to me—like the opening of a play when the curtain rises.

The action began with four huge defensive linemen in a garish simulation of Dumas' musketeers, with swirling fluorescent purple capes that magnified their expansive shoulders, spotted pantaloons above colored stockings on calves as thick as tree trunks, and platform boots that lifted them to majestic heights. It seemed like an eighteenth-century costume party of black giants missing only the swords and face masks. For want of a more sensible reaction, I found myself grinning—a sad mistake, as it turned out, for they fixed their eight eyes on me with a look so devastatingly cold and contemptuous, one would think they had seen maggots crawling over a steak at training meal.

"Sheeee-it!" snarled one, thereby recording that first word for posterity. Not merely a word, I knew, but a charged emotional expression that seemed to capsulize the gruesome dramatics of what was in store for me. Though I had always gotten along swimmingly with athletes, the notorious personality of this club was foreboding. After all, why should they bother with such an intruder as myself? Would they see me as an effete, affected snob? I had a sudden vision of their tormenting me, hazing me, even brutalizing me. Or, perhaps, a snide, denigrating, insulting mockery. My stomach fell, as they say, a ferocious reminder that this was no ordinary game I was going to play. To write a book with "Sheeee-it" for openers was no great problem. It was the fix that baffled; everything that unfolded before me, every look, every word, would be like oils splattered on canvas, layer after layer, until I could somehow create a masterpiece.

In they came, one after another in a weird passing parade. One was dressed as Santa Claus, long white-bearded and puffed with pillows. Another followed wrapped in blood-stained bandages looking like the Mummy's Revenge. Two men danced in in tandem, encased in the mangy hide of a bull, its exaggerated phallus dragging along the floor for six or seven feet. Then, curiously, another Santa who, infuriated by his rival, immediately attacked, grappling on the floor in a bullish embodiment of Christmas spirit. On went the show, the next arrival being clearly recognizable, for he was the great running back Loren "Ace" Carter, All-Pro for three successive years, the all-time All-American cocksman, currently one of New York's most celebrated bachelors. His was a furtive entrance, obviously to conceal the ghastly sight of a bleary-eyed hangover, lipstick smearing his mouth, and a rather astonishing incapacity to walk a straight line. I could even catch the rancid whisky smell of him as he closed in on the sanctuary of his locker. Of course, no one watched anything else—especially since he was crossing the door to the coach's room precisely at the wrong moment.

Coach Ike Seager stopped in his tracks, shuddering in a kind of minishock, so nervous it seemed as if *he* were the guilty one.

Carter seemed much too far gone to be worried. In fact, he was genuinely pleased to see the coach.

" 'Mornin', skipper."

"Goddammit, Carter, you look like shit warmed over!"

Carter reeled, leaning against a locker as he stared in disbelief. "Come to think of it, you don't look so hot yerself" then laughed at his comeback line with the gusto of one who had just discovered W. C. Fields.

"That'll cost you $100!"

"What! What for?"

"You're drunk, that's what for! You're so potted you can't even walk!"

"Drunk! I ain't drunk!" and Carter stared at the coach as though this were the greatest insult ever hurled at him. Then he leaned over to put his palms down on the floor, upending his body, and he began to walk on his hands, twice changing direction to avoid obstacles with never a suggestion of losing his balance. And when he righted himself, he executed a perfect flip not six inches from Seager's protruding belly—which he promptly tapped with the back of his hand.

"Jesus . . ." Seager gasped, far more flustered than amused, for the uproarious laughter in the locker room was at his expense. Humiliation, it seemed, was just another part of his job. It could even be said he was hired for his capacity to absorb it. (Some joked that Stillson had written it into his contract.) That he should get it from both ends was, of course, shameless, yet neither players nor owner appeared to think any the less of him.

He had been a decent lineman in his day, a team player, it was said of him. At sixty-five, however, he seemed more like an ex-Teamster cursed with bad kidneys and a nagging wife. That he should be the skipper of the most cantankerous team in professional football was as much an anomaly as Woody Allen playing Hamlet. As Ace Carter would put it: "He's a nice guy but he can't dance," an untranslatable quip that applied to losers. Seager was simply Stillson's tool and everyone knew it. He made no real effort to pretend otherwise, thereby not compounding his obsequiousness with hypocrisy. Stillson was the enemy. There was so much hatred for Stillson, a flunkey such as Seager seemed like a pimple on the fringes of a malignant chancre. They would have their fun picking at him and let it go at that.

For the most part, the Bulls were a motley collection of social misfits, a complete violation of the straight-square-respectable image that the official world of professional football wished of its players, principally out of deference to the TV sponsors intent on selling products. The Bulls were more like jackals, a bunch of undisciplined, contumacious rowdies who seemed to delight in breaking rules both on and off the field. Much to Commissioner Pete Rozelle's horror, it was revealed that there were four ex-cons on the squad, one of whom had actually robbed a bank. Another was a rapist. The quarterback was once an active member of the Ku Klux Klan. Still another was prominently known to have been a sexual aberrant. Two others were waived from other clubs because of alleged homosexuality.

That they should have gathered in New York was no accident. This was Lester Stillson's team. Lester had collected them because no one else would touch them. Whoever dreamed of seeing on network TV, during the first game of the season, two players from the same team emerge from a huddle viciously slugging each other like savage kids in a street brawl, a whole team, in fact, piling on as they took sides in an obviously racial clash, while 60,000 spectators—plus 50,000,000 viewers—watched agape. I had seen the replay of this travesty and, like other sophisticated fans, predicted a season of disaster, even though the Bulls managed to win that game.

Not the finest credentials, to say the least. Not a "You-gotta-believe"-type team. Yet with each victory, New York learned to accept them. First the bigots whose hearts went out to the brawlers of any stripe; even the black fans who could tolerate an avowed nigger-hater far more readily than a two-faced honky; and finally the rest of us, however muddled by this phenomenon, however ambivalent we felt toward their progress. There was fascination in each game, rising with each turbulent unpredictable victory until we swallowed our old-fashioned notions and simply enjoyed the triumphant show.

All this and more was history, and from what I would hear, even greater horrors lay buried from the public lest a scandal become overwhelming. If nothing else, the logic of the Fix became infinitely more palpable.

So, while players drifted over, I sat at the center table with all those footballs, dutifully moving the balls one by one from one end to the other as a player would sign, trying to figure out a system wherein no player would sign his name twice on the same ball. A cumbersome job, for footballs, unlike books, do not pile easily.

It wasn't until I looked at the footballs themselves that I saw a few strange signatures: Red Grange; C. Tease; Lester Sucks. And finally, a drawing of a dripping phallus. What would be the fate of these footballs, I wondered?

Not without embarrassment, I confronted Sy with them, having failed at my first assignment. He took one look at the product and quickly dropped the balls into a large duffel bag, not even bothering to count them, then whisked them away into a dark corner of his supply room.

I took a moment aside to jot down as much of this as possible, scribbling rapidly across small spiral-bound pages recreating bits of dialogue for my book. I had long since abandoned any plan to wire myself for fear that any recording device might be discovered, offending those whose candor I needed. To tape-record them openly was equally unfeasible for there were always those who refused to talk in front of a mike. Note taking, however, was respected. A writer's prerogative. In fact, his duty. It showed earnestness in quest of accuracy.

Then I looked up to see one of the most jarring sights imaginable, for in the doorway stood a grotesque transvestite, so huge it appeared unearthly, like an ogre from out of space. The face was a gargoyle smeared with rouge and excess eye shadow: scarlet lipstick exaggerated a sinister mouth; a garish blond wig made Phyllis Diller's hairdo seem demure; a sparkling midi-length silver gown under a six-foot mink stole exposed the stumpiest pair of legs I'd ever seen on animal or beast. This apparition stood there, a white-gloved hand extended along heavy hairy arms that were far too long for the squat torso, holding a jeweled cigarette holder with smoldering cigarette, limp wristed, to be sure, his right knee canted toward the left in the classic pose of a bathing beauty. The smile, abetted by fluttering lashes, was an unbelievable travesty of charm.

"Hi, there . . ." he chirped, and the roar that greeted him would have melted Bob Hope.

This was my introduction to the great Jud Kling, middle linebacker extraordinaire, the most vicious defensive player in modern football, a man who hits so hard, he once crippled a ball carrier by breaking his back on a single tackle. "A fire hydrant with legs," a sportswriter once described this body, and to expand the image, one that squirted not water but fire itself as from a dragon's mouth. If, as they say, good linebackers are born biting the obstetrician's hand, then Kling's first move had to have been a sharp kick in the doctor's gonads.

"Kling Klong," the fans would cry out from the stands when he'd come lumbering off the field after a shattering third-down tackle, but no one would ever call him that to his face.

Now he was sashaying around the room, wobbling on spiked heels as the rest of them clapped a rhythmic beat. He twitted a nose here, flicked an exposed penis there, turning the room into a night club stage with remarkable style, like one who had done this sort of thing frequently. On the second turn, he began working on his left glove, beginning a striptease, graceful and undulating and, for all his beastliness, tremendously sensual. Off came the gloves, the swirling stole; and with startling slickness, he unzipped the dress, slipped out of it without missing a beat. His bra was an inflated monstrosity of royal purple silk, his bikini panties of clashing green with yellow polka dots. Closing in on the climax, his moves became surprisingly delicate, relying on subtlety rather than exaggeration, and when he tossed his bra in the air, it was executed with such artful femininity, I found myself captivated by his talent.

Eventually, he drifted toward the table where I sat, never so much as glancing my way, the huge, muscled, hairy body continually gyrating, gradually slithering out of his bikini as gracefully as a belly dancer. He began staring at me in a way that returned all the terror to my presence. In a matter of seconds, I became a target, not an observer, for he was snapping his pelvis in that classic stripper's bump, flopping his giant genitals out inches from my face. Suddenly, then, he leaned over, grabbed my hair to control my head, forcing me to look into his open mouth as it descended to my face. Teeth, all I could see were teeth, closer and closer they came until they wrapped around my nose, my entire nose was locked in his mouth, and for a moment I actually feared that he would bite it off for he roared into my nostrils like a sick lion. I squalled in horror as my knees buckled under me, and he dropped me to the floor like a wet rag doll. I lay there breathing heavily, wondering what new atrocity was to be my fate, then I looked up at the huge buttocks as he squatted over me. On them were painted, in scarlet lipstick, my initials, "G L".

I could hear laughter ringing through the room and managed to look up at the forty-odd faces grinning at me. An initiation rite, one might call it. One of those "Welcome-to-the-NFL" sort of rituals. I even saw Lester Stillson himself, laughing as one of them, going out of his way to congratulate Kling, then using it as an excuse to ridicule me.

"I assume you've all heard about our new equipment boy. Stand up, Littlefield. Don't be scared. Stand up and let 'em all see you."

I stood up, and at the instant of rising, someone behind me timed a singularly loud fart to herald it. Naturally, a round of applause followed.

"He's a Princeton man," Lester went on. "You can tell by that pasty green look, you know?" Laughter. "They don't mind cleaning up shit, but they just don't like to hear it *said*. So maybe you guys better watch your tongue for a while. And yeah, he may need a little help every now and then—like he's apt to faint when he sees some blood out there—so don't be too hard on him."

Well, I'd assumed as much—especially from Lester, and at every opportunity. In light of my purpose, I could see where this might become troublesome.

Curiously, it took one of them to straighten me out.

He was a large freckled-faced redhead with a roly-poly Babe Ruth–sort of body. I recognized him as one of the Santas. He came at me with an outstretched hand and a big friendly grin, more like a Rotarian then a derisive Bull.

"Howdy, Mr. Littlefield, my name is Noren, Chuck Noren."

"Ah, the stalwart center," I said, and we shook hands.

"Pleased to meet you. You've got a big fan in me." And he laid a large supportive hand on my shoulder, smiling through all those freckles. "Don't let that ribbing bother you. If you really want to know, the whole damn show was put on *for you.* Everybody was saying 'Look at me!' you know what I mean?"

It was all so simple, I must have registered a momentary shock. Of course, of course. It was inevitable that the people I wrote about would become as seductive as possible when the writer was himself a celebrity. A reversal of roles, one might call it. There were occasions when I had but to present myself and the stage would be set for the badinage of hyperbolic characters and their weird capers, one seeking to outdo the others in a mad competition to be immortalized in print. Not only athletes but cooks and congressmen, yes, even fellow writers. I thrived on their antics, recording them all in my ever-present notebooks as they mugged and preened and prattled. Long ago, I had abandoned attempts to separate what was genuine and what was fabricated. Indeed, what did it matter? I merely relied on my talent to bring it all to life.

My position among them became especially evident a few minutes later. I had retreated to a relatively quiet corner of the rec room adjacent to the lockers, an area of sofas and vinyl-covered chairs, card tables, refrigerator, color TV, sport-star photographs on the wall. The TV was splaying out gunplay from a cop show rerun to which no one paid attention, it didn't matter, it was always on.

I was furiously scribbling notes, gratified that my concentration was sufficient to blot out the rival sounds when a familiar bar of music from the TV set captured my ear, then an all too familiar voice: my own.

"Hello, I'm Gordon Littlefield. . . . Let me tell you of a cherished moment in my day that I try never to miss. . . ."

I blanched, my pen scribbling on without even forming words in a spartan pose of cool indifference. A little game of I-won't-look, don't-you-look, for on that screen, I knew, was a pompous view of myself as I sat elegantly in evening clothes sipping a gold-rimmed cup of Royal British Tea, mouthing the preposterous dialogue of the huckster. A morning's work for a sizable addition to my income suddenly became thirty interminable seconds wherein I could barely catch my breath as I waited for the ridicule they would heap upon me. In my mind's eye, I saw in living color the steady hand with the saucer over crossed legs in black striped trousers, the cup's return after an agreeable taste reaction from my lips, the smile of contentment ("Yeah, like you've just fucked Racquel Welsh," the director had coached me), then the cloying peroration "I cannot think more of life's pleasures than a twilight cup of Royal British Tea (smile invitingly). Why don't you try it? (hold smile to fade-out) . . ." I looked up, prepared for a chorus of derision.

"Well, all riiiight!" exclaimed Zoad, the big redheaded fullback whom they simply called "Z."

"I'll try some . . . iced, if you don't mind," said the blond defensive back Ernie Snyder.

"I go for that dinner jacket, Gordon. Real class," added number-two quarterback Ted Monnell.

"Ah, 'life's pleasures at twilight . . .'" crooned Ace Carter. "Beautiful . . ."

I suppressed any show of relief, a testimonial to breeding and tradition, for we Littlefields were famous for rallying in a crisis. Poise was our shield, and wit was our weapon. I stood up, and with the humility of all great men, accepted their applause.

What quickly became apparent was that the thirty-second exposure was the hallmark of a true celebrity. That they must have seen it before was irrelevant. To see it in my presence was the *sine qua non* of my acceptability. After all, I was not an actor, I was a real writer, a personality. To them, a commercial was a status symbol, the summit of their careers, reserved for the Joe Namaths and O. J. Simpsons. It was not only a reward for achievement on the field, but a stepping-stone to new plateaus, an exposure to be envied as much as anything they did on the gridiron. I was, then, their peer. Not a slumming Princeton parasite, not a mere sportswriter, certainly, but a national figure who was pleased to associate with them.

It was, then, a fine morning for a fixer.

Was I not harnessing the power of an idea whose time had come?

8

Friday (Nine Days to Go)

The extravagance of my opening day experience diminished to a plodding routine as the week progressed. For the players, the concentration was mainly on films of their Superbowl rivals, the Dallas Cowboys. The club met daily and divided into groups, offense and defense, retreating to separate rooms to study their opponents in action, withholding the serious physical work until Tuesday in Los Angeles wherein the normal practice procedures would build toward Sunday's game.

For me, every day was made up of countless experiences and confrontations, all of them grist for my mill. I was a diligent and relentless observer, picking up bits and pieces of information wherever I went. Ever conscious of passing time and the need to move as rapidly as possible, I nonetheless assumed the posture of one who was exactly the opposite. I concentrated on getting the feel of this club, a sense of its dominant personalities. I listened, watched the action flow around me. I got to know them as individuals.

The prospects intrigued me, for everything I did became part of my schema, even the hours spent with Sy, for he was an endless fountain of gossip about the club.

Sy was a dynamo on the sidelines, a tornado in the locker room. His diligence over the most miniscule detail was absolute, everything checked and rechecked. One would think this week was a countdown to a space shot. I told him of my admiration, adding that the world needed more of him, and I was pleased to see him loosen up as a result. But he gave me no quarter when it came to doling out chores, one of which was the daily replacement of brand-new white laces in Lester Stillson's ripple-soled coach's shoes, worn at daily practice as he moved among the formations like a czar.

"*Every* day?" I asked in amazement.

The explanation was simple enough, duly reported here for its illumination of character: Stillson had once broken a lace as he'd tied it, something that might happen to anyone at one time or another, but Lester alone would take it personally. A devious plot on his well-being, no doubt, malevolently conceived by a dissident employee who'd deliberately shaved it just enough to break under pressure.

He saw I was an earnest worker (I was seen discarding a torn jock) and began to warm up a bit. On the third day, he was telling me stories about everything from chin straps to tackling dummies, all items within his province, stopping only to count this or that when necessary.

"Short practice, long press conference," Sy advised me on Friday morning. "You're gonna see a lot of hair spray in here today," commenting on the photographers due in. "This place'll look like a big TV commercial and smell like a barber shop."

"Well, there's certainly a lot of hair on this club."

"Gets longer every year. I'm waiting for a kid like Snyder to intercept and get tackled by the hair a few yards from the goal."

Cornerback Ernie Snyder's hair extended well below the back of his helmet. Such a tackle did not seem out of the question, I thought. It did seem incredible that a pro would risk it, but such is the price of vanity.

"Well, I don't suppose it matters very much," I said.

"The hell you say!" he barked. "We've had *two* drain stoppages in the shower. Had to rip up pipes to clean 'em out. Big balls of hair coagulated in there. Trouble is, some of these guys are beginning to grow bald."

"Must be a few hairpieces around," I offered.

"A bald jock would have a tougher time than a nigger before Jackie Robinson," he agreed, then shook his head, chortling at a sudden memory. "Ernie Snyder shampoos those golden locks every day with a kit full of junk. He's got three hair dryers going at different temperatures, then he sprays all the crap on and combs it for an hour. Look at his locker: there's *four* mirrors in there! One day I says to him: 'Ernie, I got bad news for you: you're the type that's gonna be bald.' Well, he spins around terrified, then he says: 'I'd rather lose two inches of cock!' "

So ended the discussion about hair.

It was a mark of Sy's faith in me that he put me in charge of the footballs. All sixteen of the practice balls. They had to be thoroughly cleaned after each practice and periodically checked at the air pressure gauge. "*Thirteen* pounds. Not twelve and a half, not thirteen and a half. The number is thirteen," he said.

"Does it really matter *that* much?"

The question pleased him, a chance to show his superior knowledge. "You put a ball out there off the number and watch a quarterback scowl. Stonewall, he puts a hand on it and he *knows*. And the kicker, Grazlov, that sidewinder from 'Slavia . . . he once kicked one from the forty and it went a little high, so when it came back, he threw it away, he didn't want to kick it again. I checked it out: it was almost one under the number!"

I also had to control the flow of balls during practice. Sixteen out, sixteen back. Two canvas bags of eight. "That'll be your job at the Bowl," he advised me. "Pregame practice, you gotta have eyes all over you. It's a time of confusion, you can be sure of that. A time of confusion is a time of thieves."

"*Inside* the L.A. Coliseum?"

"There are a zillion kids floating around the field with press armbands and cameras coming out their A-holes, and they'll steal anything. Hell, I once saw a kid come from behind in the middle of the game and steal the hairpiece off an injured player when they propped him on the bench!"

"What would he want with a wig?"

"Souvenir, I guess. I tell you, it'll be a madhouse out there. You get them balls in the bag, you tie 'em shut, whatever happens, take 'em straight to the locker room, and hang on as you go 'cause they'll be watching you. If necessary, you can swing the bag, it's a weapon, you know. You can get pretty good speed going and it comes down heavy enough."

That very afternoon, returning to the parking lot with Ace and Chuck Noren after a few beers, I saw Sy coming out of the stadium with the familiar canvas bag, obviously full of footballs. It had to be those autographed balls, I thought. Collectors' items, no doubt, worth $100 a piece, perhaps. Two hundred dollars if these salacious inscribers became Superbowl champs.

Sy, Sy, is this really *your* style too? Even as I toyed with so misanthropic a notion, I sensed it was so. It was a den crawling with thieves as well as cutthroats. The details were as fascinating as the concept itself. I would revel in them, soaking up the stories of interminable viciousness and disharmony.

"You remember the famous huddle fight, pal?" Ace said in the gin mill across from the stadium. "You wouldn't believe that day. Right from the time old Stonewall got in the game, he goes on the fucking warpath. 'Power 21, pinch block,' he calls, 'and you fucking pit niggers better do your job! On three, on three!' Imagine a quarterback saying that! And when he throws passes, it's just to Z and me, us whiteys, and none to Gil Warner or Willie Jones, the blacks, or even to Coley Barone, you know, the pervert. Once, Buck Hoover lets his man beat him on a pass play—maybe deliberately, I don't know—and Stonewall gets nailed for a heavy loss. 'You fucking nigger,' he says, 'you couldn't stop my grandmother 'less you had a knife in your hand!' By the middle of the second quarter, the game is 7–7, Gil is seething. You can see the steam coming out of his eyes. 'I'm open,' he says. 'I'll fake outside and go to the post. I'm gone, I tell you. I'm *gone*!' But Stonewall says to him: 'I wouldn't waste a play on a nigger. You got butter for hands and shit for blood.' And that's when Gil blew up. He goes at Stonewall like a damn wildcat. I tell you, he was so mad there was no way to pull him off."

"What happened then?" I asked.

"Two plays later, Stonewall calls the fake screen and throws it to Gil, just like Gil asked, and just like Gil said, he was gone. Stonewall puts it on the money and it goes for six."

"Did he say anything later?"

"Yeah. He said he'd play with niggers but he wouldn't talk to them."

"There's precious little love in this outfit," said Chuck.

"What about Kling?" I asked later. "Does anyone mess with him?"

"Only his wife," Chuck replied.

"Oh? What's she like?"

He laughed. "Like what you saw in drag."

"What!"

"She really goes at him. She won't take *any*thing from him. We used to kid about it, behind his back, you know, like maybe if he gets hurt, *she* can take his place, that sort of thing. But it got too dangerous. I mean, one morning, he came in with a large shiner and a cracked lip and no one said a *word!*"

"Let's face it, he's mean," Ace went on. "That's one of the things that makes him so great out there. He's a linebacker, pal. Attila the Hun was a linebacker. Frankenstein was a linebacker until he tore his Achilles tendon. The Boston Strangler was a linebacker in high school. You shoulda seen Kling take on three rookies during the summer. Wow!"

"He fought *three!*"

"To a standstill, I swear, the ground was shaking like a stampede of buffalo."

"Why? What caused it?"

"They were *line*backers trying for his job," Ace said. "Kling is unmerciful to rookies, pal. He just can't stand them."

"But he's so great! Surely, nobody's going to take *his* job!" I said.

"The man is what they call 'insecure.' Maybe his mother was a tough toilet trainer or he wasn't allowed to play with his wang, who knows?"

It was a difficult premise to accept, just as it was difficult to think of Kling as ever having been a baby.

"Maybe one day I'll get to talk to him," I said.

"You gotta come at him *low* key, pal," Ace advised. "Take two Valiums and a pheno-barb, and talk real soft-like. . . ."

I laughed and promised that I would.

9
Sunday (Seven Days to Go)

On this Sunday morning, I felt a boyish contentment in weariness, having risen at dawn to assist Sy at the stadium in the final packing and loading of equipment, 2500 pounds of it, then trucking it to the airport, a dozen huge trunks full of football gear, all labeled and checked out, piece by piece, up the conveyer belt and into the gaping hold. And when the last item disappeared, Sy checked his watch, nodded, almost managing to smile.

"Not bad for a Princeton man," he said.
"Maybe I should ask Stillson for a raise."
"Last guy who did ended up in the Harlem River."

And so we were on our way to Los Angeles for the final big week, a chartered 707 loaded with five tons of football players, a ton of coaches, medics and trainers, and another ton of freeloading newspapermen. I sat safety belted by a rear window, fantasizing on the drama that was in store for me. My view of the sprawling suburbs was erased by cloudcover, climbing over thick billowing cotton beds that lent itself to all manner of speculations.

It had been a good week wherein I had made substantial progress. The book-in-work was obviously loaded with colorful characters and diverting incidents, and there would doubtlessly be more, much more, in the drama of the oncoming days to Sunday. This gratified me, not only as another illustration of my talents, but for the artistry with which I had established my dual role (after all, I mused, you can't tell a man's cover by his book), having blessed myself with an extraordinary paradox wherein the more questions I asked, the less suspicious anyone was likely to be.

Nonetheless, I lived with an underlying tension. Since I was not there to write, except for show, I was faced with a curious switch, for I had always assumed roles for show in order to write of them. The implications of this contradiction were not lost on me; in fact, I found them challenging enough. To illustrate: I'd had no difficulty in such role-playing actions as goalie for the Boston Bruins hockey team (an exhibition game) because the players were all part of the act. What I would dramatically describe as a test of courage with hard rubber pucks flying at vital organs at 120 miles an hour was actually no such thing. It would be a test of nothing but my ability to write, for the hockey players were *not* my competitors, they were *not* trying to defeat me, quite the contrary, they were using all their skills to make me look good.

And therein lay the meat of my current problem. For the first time, except for Patricia, I had no real allies. There would be no role playing when it actually came down to fixing the game. This time, I had to *do* something and do it alone. This time, I would have to face danger.

What intrigued me was that I found enjoyment in the challenge. A week before, I'd suffered the stifling impact of my fortieth birthday. I now sensed a greater exhilaration than I'd ever known.

It followed that I could hardly indulge myself in a transcontinental nap. Plane trips were designed for inquiring journalists—as demonstrated by the dozen New York area newspapermen aboard, also guests of the Bulls' management. I knew a few of them slightly. There was Ben Cooperman, senior sportswriter for the *Times*, who'd covered the Bulls for years. Nice man, uninspired writer. Read his column and one would think Lester Stillson was a golden-hearted public benefactor behind an unfortunately severe facade. And his opposite, Joe Weed of the *Post*, that glib cynic to whom the name Lester Stillson was an outright obscenity. So much so, in fact, that his presence on this plane was somewhat astonishing for Lester had twice barred him from the Bulls' locker room.

"Yeah, Joe, how come you made it?" I asked him.

"My sainted mother wrote him for permission," he said. Then: "How do I know how come! I don't give a damn one way or the other. There's a dozen flights a day, right?" And, in the same breath: "Christ Almighty, Littlefield, aren't you sick of writing those bullshit books?"

"They pay the rent."

"Rent! You must own half the East Side by now."

Joe Weed was something, all right.

Quickly enough, the cabin turned into a social club. Groups formed for card games—gin in the seats, poker in the club compartment. Two stewardesses circulated, so much so, it was difficult to tell who was on the make for whom. Others gathered in pockets for routine talk. Some sat alone, reading magazines. Etore Wisting, the eccentric linebacker, uncased his guitar and was singing folk songs and country music along with a few of the faithful. The rednecked quarterback, Stonewall Jackson, was eternally terrified of flying, it seemed, and like a recluse, curled up in his seat wearing earplugs and, believe it or not, blinders. By tradition, he never moved, never spoke, did not eat or drink. No signs of life until the wheels touched earth again. An interior lineman named Perry Lee Stover, wearing steel-rimmed glasses, was reading a frayed leather-bound Bible, his lips moving slowly as if in prayer.

My first friend, the redheaded center ("Call me Chuck"), continued to be solicitous.

"What sort of book this gonna be, Gordon?"

I explained that I really didn't know yet, it would depend on how well I got to know which players, what actually happened, and so forth. He seemed genuinely interested, then humbly indicated how far beyond his capacities such talents were.

"I don't think I'd be much good playing center," I said.

"I'll bet a lot more people can play football than write a book." His modesty was highly ingratiating.

"Chuck, you sound like a happy man," I offered.

"That's me, all right. No complaints—'less you consider a rotten salary, the way I was cheated on a bonus last year, a couple of juicy fines this year, and maybe a half dozen bullshit grievances."

"Sounds normal enough around here."

"Oh, you'll hear some beauts," he admitted. "We used to have a sign over the locker room door: 'Thru this portal pass the World's Biggest Suckers.'"

"The Home of the Damned," I said.

"When you're fucked by Lester, you're fucked by the bester," he sing-sang. At first amused by the familiar sound of it, he suddenly reversed himself, driving his fist into the seat in front of him with astonishing ferocity, his face turning instant scarlet to complement his rage. As quickly as this engulfed him, it washed away, and he laughed at himself and slapped my knee.

"As my daddy used to say: 'Fuck 'em all, big and small.'"

"I daresay, you'll survive, Chuck," I commended him.

He nodded. "Write a good book, Gordon," he replied, and he made it sound important that I did.

I liked him.

I wandered among them, stopping here and there. The atmosphere was friendly and loose what with Stillson and the brass in the first class cabin. I found myself welcomed everywhere, except for the militant black cornerback Henry Coll.

"You smell something cruddy, Oscar? All of a sudden, it reeks 'round here."

He was no ordinary-looking man with his vast Afro, his scarred face flaring anger through a fierce Fu Manchu moustache. Henry was a mean one, all right, and a reputation for being a cheap shot artist on the field. Extremely aggressive, he would hurt a vulnerable receiver in the first few plays to establish intimidation, then provoke him with petty insults, even spitting at him. Anything to upset his concentration. Far tougher than most, and totally fearless, he was extremely effective—and grossly disliked. He seemed to thrive on animosity.

He glared at me, but spoke to Oscar Ayers, a safety, also black.

"Don't fuck with him, brother," he said, persisting in the pretense that I wasn't really there. "He's a stooge for the Man, ain't he. Why else would Lester let him in. He makes his bundle writing books about us, and we get nothing. If he wants you to talk, make him pay."

"Aw, cool it, Henry," Oscar said.

"He writes about how great the system is, brother. He don't know for shit!"

"Last I heard, the money was fairly good," I interjected.

"Blacks are better, get paid less. Every brother knows that."

"O. J. Simpson gets less?" I asked.

"*Half* what Namath made!"

He was so angry at this point, he openly acknowledged my existence. "You know about Oscar in college?" he asked me. "You know that Oscar was the finest quarterback ever to hit Texas football? You know Oscar's record?"

"No . . ." I confessed.

"He come to New York and old Lester says: 'No, QB, you DB. We don't go for nigger QB's.' Sheee-it, Oscar was the motherfucking greatest, but they tell him he's *lucky* to make the squad."

Henry grunted, implying that my ignorance was no surprise to him at all. He turned back to Oscar, reverting to his earlier posture.

"Don't talk to him."

Someone laughed, but not with any enthusiasm.

"That true what he said about you?" I asked Oscar.

"You can look it up."

I looked at Oscar, a seven-year veteran, still lean and hard as nails, a short, curly, face-covering beard to accentuate his blackness. He had small grey eyes that smiled but not with any particular friendliness. At least not to me. A verbal counterpuncher, one might say. A hard man, I thought, but worth pursuing. After all, I *was* looking for bitterness. Bitterness was the primary force behind any sensibly conceived fix. Greed, too. But in my estimation, greed was secondary. Ideally, I wanted to find two men who'd be ready to throw this game for nothing.

"Oscar, is playing football fun for you?"

He eyed me curiously as though the question were loaded with dangerous implications.

"A lot better'n working in a woolen mill."

"Is that your alternative?"

"It's what my brothers do."

"Are you going back there when you quit football?"

"Hell, no. I'm gonna buy the Bulls from old Lester!"

Others laughed.

Later, I would learn that his wife was divorcing him. What with child support for two infants and, no doubt, substantial alimony payments, he would be in a nasty financial bind—a problem that apparently needled him badly.

I liked that.

I didn't get two rows away when I was flagged down by linebacker Jake Kolacka, a cigarette dangling from his lips.

"Old Henry work you over?" he asked.

"The dregs of four hundred years of racism," I nodded. "He's got a point, you know."

"But you got a better one," and he pointed to the tip of my pen.

Not bad for openers. We had never spoken before, but there was no need for introductions. The mutual recognition factor took care of everything. I sat down on the seat beside him, and he put aside his *Playboy*.

It was immediately apparent that he was not currying favor. He was a genuine article, and a strange one with a bizarre history to go with his well-publicized 141 IQ. Several years before he had pulled off a lucrative bank robbery with a toy gun, then turned himself in, amusing himself with all the psychiatric probing of so-called experts both in and out of mental institutions.

"I suppose you heard I was a bank robber, and all that craziness," he said. "The shrinks called it a schizophrenic reaction, that I didn't know what I was doing. I was acquitted. NGI, Not Guilty by Reason of Insanity." He laughed. "Do I seem insane to you?"

"No," I admitted, "Not at all." Then I challenged him. "But that doesn't mean that you aren't."

"True enough. And I *could* act it up for you, I made a study of it. All the symptoms: incoherent speech, inner voices, constantly changing the subject, even the repeated use of adjectives like horrendous, catastrophic, terrifying. . . . Shit, I can fake out a shrink any time I want!"

He told it straight out. No shame, no embarrassment. It

was as though it were all no more serious than playing hookey from high school. He was amused by the telling, perhaps even proud of it. The whole thing smacked of such amorality, I felt a twinge of excitement.

He never took his eyes from me. "Oh, I'm a character, all right. The consummate football player: body of a fullback, brain of a quarterback, psyche of a wide receiver."

The wide receiver reference was interesting since they were supposed to be different. Loners, way out there on the flank. Some of them *were* strange, I was told, sort of like oboe players in a symphony orchestra. However, it was the NGI part I appreciated the most. It suggested daring, irreverence, deceit. One could talk enterprisingly to a man like Kolacka.

Later, I noticed a crowd had gathered around the quiet Bible-reading lineman, Perry Lee Stover. Not surprisingly, the provocateur was the ubiquitous Jake Kolacka, who persisted in laying pornographic photographs on the open pages of Perry Lee's Bible. Almost as quickly as Perry Lee discarded one, a new one was inserted.

"Hey, Perry Lee, here's a hot one of Adam and Eve."

"They say Eve was one helluva cocksucker. Is that right, Perry Lee?"

"That's the *New* Testament," suggested another.

"Hey, here's one where Eve gets fucked by a gorilla!"

Oh, they got Perry Lee to look, all right. For all his indignant protests, one could hardly expect him to resist indefinitely. Furtively, he would glance at a picture, half-shutting the Bible as though to screen its sacred words from such obscene sights, and Kolacka would literally pummel him with added erotica. "Look at that golden ass, Perry Lee . . . flesh as clean and firm as God could possible create it . . . just made for a Godlike phallus made stiff by a loving God-given passion. . . . And, lookit, Perry Lee, here they are, the two golden lovers in a celestial arbor, look at that voluptuous body rising off the sweet-scented lush green grass to receive him. . . . God, it's beautiful, beautiful. . . ."

At which Perry Lee could tolerate the strain no longer, pushing up from the seat to shoulder his way by them all, hurrying to the privacy of the lavatory.

Kolacka laughed, tossed the photos in the air to celebrate his triumph, then extended his open hand toward the others. "Even money for the hard-on. Two to one for masturbation."

They paid up, fives and tens, and Kolacka could not resist gloating, catching my eye with an exaggerated wink. When the party broke up, he added up his ill-gotten winnings, obviously very pleased with himself.

"Fifty-five bucks. Not a bad stunt."

"The devil's work," I teased him.

"Ah, but not without consent of the disciple," he grinned, then leaned across the seat for the Bible, opened it to the ribbon-marker, quickly inserted two fives.

"A bloody conspiracy!" I could hardly conceal my surprise.

He winked again, very proudly, I might add.

"And I thought he was a true believer," I said.

"Oh, he loves God, all right. But he loves money more."

"And you?" I asked. "What motivates you?"

"Inka dinka doo, a-dinka dee, a-dinka doo . . ." He sang that old Jimmy Durante song, a total non sequitur, but it would have to do.

It was all so incredible, I had to wait around to see the finale, placing myself a few rows away with a convenient angle to Perry Lee's seat. It was perhaps ten minutes before he returned, working his way down the aisle as though nothing had happened. He dropped his muscular body slowly into his seat, returned his glasses to his face, reopened the Bible. A cautious move, I noted, and unquestionably prepared for the blessing he was about to receive. His hand quickly palmed the bills as he began reading, lips moving as he scanned the half-width biblical columns. It wasn't until he turned the page that he pocketed the money, furtively withdrawing a handkerchief to mask the move—just in case someone was watching.

Having let me in on such deviously conceived erotica, I was not surprised when they approached me on a more functional spin-off. Curiously, it wasn't the wily Kolacka this time, but the big defensive tackle, Tiny LaTourette, with the golden-haired cornerback Ernie Snyder in tow.

"We got this idea for a movie, Gordon," Tiny began. "We were wondering, maybe you know some movie people in Hollywood, maybe you could help us set it up. We could make a fortune, you know?"

"What sort of movie, Tiny?"

"Well, it would show the football stars having a party. You film the party, see. We get Ace and Kling and maybe even Barone, and we show what they do off the field."

"What *do* they do?"

"Well, we have this orgy. Us big studs and a few fine little starlets. I mean, think of it, Gordon, we'll show everyone what a great cocksman Ace Carter is. And who wouldn't wanna see the film of Kling jabbing some gorgeous blonde. You know, Beauty and the Beast! You could write us a little story, maybe, to give it class. I mean, it's gotta be a winner, right? Especially after we take the Superbowl."

I told him I'd think about it.

And I did, all the way to the rear where the newspaper men were playing poker. Joe Weed had to laugh at the story.

"It goes with the altitude," he quipped. "Some of these farmers get lightheaded at 35,000 feet . . . all that air beneath them upsets them."

"I noticed they don't talk football."

"Jesus, no. Sex, more sex, and occasionally money."

"LaTourette was combining them."

"We're flying over Vegas, that's why."

I smiled. "It's not a bad idea, when you get right down to it."

"There's a better one that actually happened. On flight, too. And this one has the classic great black cock and pink-white pussy. Rollie St. Clair, the master stud, some say with the largest black tool in the NFL— which does little to endear him to his horny teammates—takes a hankering for a pretty white stewardess, and before you know it, he's got her going with him to the lavatory back there. But not for long, as it turns out, because maybe 2000 pounds of redneck defenders of lily-white womanhood come charging down the aisle to break down that door, only to face another 2000 pounds of militant black muscle. I tell you, Gordon, there was a struggle as ferocious as a goal-line stand. The plane was shaking with it; it was scary, all right."

"What happened?"

"Another stew ran to the cockpit and told the captain, and he put the big jet into a dive, zingo, and all those bodies broke loose like pins in a bowling alley. You can't fuck or fight under those conditions."

"One big happy family . . ."

"I wouldn't mind seeing film of what went on *in*side that lavatory."

In the rear of the plane, a group of players were talking about dreams. Ace Carter, the most garrulous, was obviously also the most prolific dreamer.

"They run in streaks with me. Mostly, I get the Heavy Feet Dream. Jesus, I can never get off that one fast enough! What happens is, I'm running for my life but I can hardly lift 'em."

"I get the Hands Dream," said flanker Gil Warner. "I lose my hands."

"What!"

"Yeah, they just disappear. I see the football coming, I got my man beat, all I gotta do is reach out and grab it, but I have no hands! The ball just falls through my arms."

We were approaching the giant smog bed that hovered over the Los Angeles basin, tilting in farewell to Las Vegas in a gentle turn to the south. Suddenly, the overhead speakers were alive with the sound of Lester Stillson's voice.

All right, men, it's time to get with it. I want you all cleaned up for landing. I want all that hair combed and clothes in proper condition. This is a championship football team and we will look like one. There'll be a crowd of fans at the airport; press, photographers, television. The way to get off to a proper start is to look like winners. Is that clear?

"I wake up," Gil went on as though Stillson did not exist. "First thing, I look to see if my hands are there."

"I used to dream about some guy stopping me around the legs," Ace was saying, "and Kling gets my head in his arms and twists it off. I mean, he's on my own team but he really takes my head off!"

I warn you, men, I personally will watch every one of you disembark, and if anyone is not properly dressed, it will cost him $200!

"There's a pile-up and I can't move," Ace continued. "I can't see. I can't do anything. I ain't got a head! I don't believe the damn dream, but it scares hell outta me."

Men, I want to remind you all that every move you make, every word you speak will reflect on this great club. I don't want to see anyone break discipline, and just to be sure that no one does, punishment will be imposed on all *of you!*

"You guys must be sick," said Z, the redheaded fullback. "I dream of happiness beyond compare. I have one, when it starts, I can't wait to get it going, 'cause it's always the same. I get a call for a power play, but when I hit, there ain't no hole. It don't stop me, though. I start juking and faking and pumping, crossing the backfield two, three times, all those big boogie linemen huffing after me, and I can hear the crowd screaming. Then I see the opening, and I take off like OJ himself, holding the ball out there like I don't have a care in the world, and I go downfield, snake-hipping in seven different gears, and nobody can bring me down, nobody. I'm laughing like hell as I go in for the six, and I'm actually *walking!*"

The Superbowl does not begin next Sunday: it begins the minute you step off the plane. So get cracking, men. Is that clear?

Ace thought about it. "I guess I must be nuts at that. I never dream of glory, it's always something *bad* happening, they're always destroying my body. Sometimes, I'm afraid to go to sleep. I mean, Jesus, how do you *do* it?"

"Easy. You just start your dream *before* you go to sleep," Z said.

Actually, Stillson's words on appearance were totally unnecessary, for there was hardly a professional group in America more conscious of the way it looked at all times —both on and off the field. The cabin storage was loaded with clothes bags, lockers above seats with attaché cases full of cosmetics. Everyone carried a pocket comb. To command a football player to look neat was like commanding a fish to swim.

Ernie Snyder of the long blond tresses had a stewardess holding a pocket mirror while he combed himself.

"I'm getting ready for kickoff," he said.

10

Monday (Six Days to Go)

I happen to like Los Angeles. Though I am reluctant to admit it to friends, I find a light-hearted pleasure in its outlandish domination by the motion picture and television industry—a cultural phenomenon wherein the most absurd matters are treated with reverence by otherwise intelligent and sometimes erudite adults. I seemed to roll well with the tides in L.A. I certainly had no occasion to resist them. Only a fool would walk into a whorehouse expecting to find religion.

In a way, it was the perfect setting for the sort of manipulations I was about to undertake. In this ambience, there was something almost bland about fixing the Superbowl. Just another Hollywood extravaganza. I could almost hear a dozen typewriters clicking away by swimming pools in cantilevered canyon homes, inspired by the coming game, creating wild scenarios based on exactly the same premise. To motion picture makers, every major event was a potential melodrama. A leading Hollywood writer I knew, an extremely erudite man named Neal Harkevy kept his library rich in the classic literature of perversion and crime together with the fashionable bestselling trash that glorified it. There was something outlandish about seeing Dostoevski and Spillane side by side. Or Camus and Jacqueline Suzanne. He was a writer capable of adapting *Moby Dick* one month and *Suck My Cock* the next.

I could fantasize the dialogue of my coming visit:
Say, Gordon, you working on something out here?
Well, I'm planning to fix the Superbowl game.
Not a bad idea. I have a treatment on it over at Paramount.
No, I mean, I'm really *going to fix it.*
The trouble I had getting women into the action!
Not me. You won't believe this, but . . .
They want Walter Matthau for the gambler, but he's busy. I've been trying to get Woody Allen to read it, but he prefers his own stuff.
I see, it's a comedy.
Why not? There's no heavy violence in it.

Perhaps Harkevy had the right idea. A Marx Brothers romp with halfbacks tossing banana peels at their pursuers' feet, and punt returners hiding the ball under their jerseys. Didn't the whole thing border on the farce? What were people like Lester Stillson, Kling, Kolacka, myself even, if not zany characters in a Hollywood movie? Was not the entire scenario as I envisaged it "larger than life" as they say out here?

Harkevy got started talking about the game itself, pontificating about the greatness of the Bulls.

"Finest defense in modern football history," he said.

"Oh, I don't rate them that highly," I countered. "From what little I've seen, I'm actually inclined to think Dallas is a stronger team."

He laughed quickly, shaking his head to show disdain.

"You people with inside information always amuse me," he went on. "Really, Gordon, I'm surprised at *you*."

That all this came from a pretentious screenwriter of extremely dubious credits—and enormous financial success—added fuel to my resentment. He was a heavy gambler, I knew. Poker, horses, football. I could even assume he was deliberately baiting me into betting against him. The entire scene riled me so, I had all I could do to resist exploiting it.

The next six days to Sunday would be spent, for the most part, at the Glendale Arms Motor Inn, far enough from the fleshpots of the Sunset Strip, west of Hollywood, to be inconvenient for the raunchy—yet near enough to be a tease. Practices would be held at Occidental College, a few miles from the Inn. Curfew for the players was a stringent eleven P.M., and I speculated on how it would be observed. What amused me was the way the blandness of this setting served as counterpoint to the turbulent emotions of the gridiron—like raw melodrama with a background score by Muzak.

As part of the Bulls organization, my room was among the players', lending easy access to them all—exactly as I'd wished. My only problem was the $100,000 cash I had carried with me, deftly secreted under a false bottom of my attaché case. The case, I decided, would best remain with me, in my room, left casually on the top shelf of my closet with a few nondescript PR releases if anyone should be probing among my things. Occasionally, I would pull it down to check the cash, taking pleasure in thoughts of Patricia as I did, wondering when, and if, she were coming to L.A. Indeed, I would fondle the neat piles of money, amused at my erotic memories when I did.

It was never out of mind that I had but six days left, and major decisions to make well before Sunday. I was developing an overall feel for the team, a sense of its strengths and weaknesses. I already had ideas and preferences as to possible choices. I felt no doubts about my abilities nor did

I foresee any complications. In fact, the entire project was moving so smoothly, I told myself to be wary.

So, in the privacy of my room at the Arms, I celebrated the arrival in Los Angeles by my first direct attack on the Bulls roster. Forty-three names. On the coffee table that would serve as my work space, I laid the flip card that listed them, offense on one side, defense on the other. Immediately, I eliminated all but twenty-two, eleven regulars on both sides. I could go beyond that, crossing out seven more on offense purely by position: quarterback, two running backs, two wide receivers, plus two kickers. A simple decision, for I did not want to deal with openly exposed ball handlers. Not merely because of the exposure, I might add, but because of its impact on their personalities. Such men are different. The quarterback, in particular, is a team leader by training. He is aware of his charismatic image both to teammates and to his audience. He knows he is the Main Man around whom everything revolves, that TV cameras are focused on his every move. He has always been a man apart, right from pre–high school days. He is the most recognized, the most photographed and written about, and the best paid. He even gets first crack at the most beautiful girls. All this is part of his tradition and he thinks accordingly. Less so, but in the same vein, are the running backs. Some super stars like O. J. Simpson and Ace Carter might even surpass the quarterback in these qualities. The others, the receivers, are prima donnas in their own smaller way, all victims of the classic pecking order, but they tend to have this one singular quality in common: a self-awareness as the center of attention.

Such men were simply not apt to lend themselves to the ignominy of a poor performance.

But a man buried "in the trenches," a "horse" whose Sundays consist of sixty or more dreary, slugging, head-to-head pileups, the details of which are rarely seen, such a man could appreciate the opportunity I would offer, if only as a way to assuage the frustration of all those years being second fiddle to the ball carrier's prestige. There were six of them to choose from, and from what I could see, some—like the amiable center, Chuck Noren—were beauts.

As for the defense, the problems of elimination were totally different. Only one was a standout, the middle linebacker, a position that might be called the quarterback of the defense with all its accompanying psychopathology. Since it was also filled by Jud Kling, I immediately excluded it from any further consideration.

Another cross-out was left tackle Alex Henderson, a big, grizzly white sadist who walked around with an icy smile and an insidious cackle reminiscent of psychotic roles played by the young Richard Widmark. He impressed me as having been the small town bully who loved every minute of the torment he inflicted. On this lineup, however, he was no longer dominant, so he resorted to wiliness or, at least, the sneering show of it. His violent eruptions off the field had become legendary, especially when drinking. He appeared to get his kicks turning over VW's with women drivers, just to hear them scream. I would be wise to let the bear have his honey.

Then there was Henry Coll, the black militant cornerback whose hatred of the whitey in me precluded any intimate dialogue. I would not dream of inviting him to my home for dinner.

On the other side of the line, the black Lem Bow, a nervous type for so big a man, extra sensitive, it seemed, and extremely unreliable. Apparently, he had a penchant for shoplifting—and getting caught—that sent him to jail on several occasions. I didn't appreciate his shifty unpredictable style. It simply did not go with his bulk. I needed a hawk, not an oversized weasel.

Beside him, at right end, was Sonny Payson, a sad, stammering, demented Texan who appeared to giggle a lot. He had such an insipid quality, I was immediately and forever repelled by him.

I could go on for a few more such eliminations, but I did not care to overplay my hand. At this point, I contented myself by taking a more theoretical bent.

For example, if one could define my ideal prospect, he would be a veteran in his last year or so, whom Stillson had swindled on a contract or broken a promise of a bonus, who felt he had never been paid up to his value, who was essentially honest yet believed $50,000 in payment for retribution was a justifiably earned farewell-to-football bonus. Add to that the blackness of his skin and, presto, the archetype.

A simple enough formula, yet each man had his own fragility. And how could I be certain of him? After all, I had my own preferences, some of which violated every premise of the above. An intuitive reaction, if you will, but eminently deserving of attention.

Take Etore Wisting, for example, the rather strange guitar-playing linebacker with his shaggy look and offbeat lifestyle. His name alone was a teaser. ("I like my name," he had told me in delightful understatement: "You don't meet many people with a name like that.") Certainly not linebackers. Great linebackers are savages like Kling. They have names like Butkus, Lucci, Nitschke, Huff. They drink straight sourmash, eat raw beef, spit nails. They watch cop shows on TV, read only sports pages and ogle nude pictures in porno magazines. Wisting, however, was none of these. He read poetry, even wrote some. He was an irreverent counterculture freak who spent his winters Jesus bearded as a wistful bachelor combing the beaches of lower California in a seedy panel truck. One could readily assume all manner of behavior possible with Etore. He might even love the challenge of the fix and turn in a masterful performance wherein he would subtly destroy the checks and balances of the entire defensive unit and come out looking like a star.

I found myself picturing a quiet beer with Wisting in the rear booth of a tavern after practice. The usual Littlefield approach for an interview. And there, the posing of the problem.

LITTLEFIELD: Etore, have you ever thought about what would happen to Stillson if you guys lost the game?

WISTING: He'd likely fly up his own asshole. A fart going backward. Jesus, how I'd love to cork that one!

LITTLEFIELD: One sometimes looks for a moment of defeat in hopes of seeing that man cry.

WISTING: It sure is piss-ant time when we win. That pompous fuck in the locker room acting like it was him making all the tackles.

LITTLEFIELD: Whereupon you pour a few more ounces of champagne on his oily head.

WISTING: I'd like to shove that head in a toilet. Ha! Stillson in the *real* Superbowl.

LITTLEFIELD: The trouble is, you won't . . . victory creates is own enchantment. There are no recriminations in victory.

WISTING: Yeah, you're right about that.

LITTLEFIELD: Etore, suppose, just suppose, someone were to give you an envelope. You get a quiet moment all to yourself, and you open it up. There's a bundle of money in it, say, a hundred and fifty $100 bills. The understanding is, on Sunday, you have a marvelous time out there, you make incredible tackles, knock down passes, smother the quarterback, the works. But you consider the rhythms of the game, the ebb and flow of its momentum, and ever so subtly, *you* see to it that they *do* score. Once, twice, whatever is necessary to upset the balance. You *lose* the game, and then on Sunday evening, there's another envelope, this time with *three* hundred and fifty $100 bills. A total of $50,000, tax free, and the pleasure of washing Stillson's head in the toilet.

WISTING: Gordon, I swear, you look like a stuffy bastard and you talk like a fucking English prince, but I just can't make any sense of this. I mean, I didn't even hear you, not one motherfucking piss-ass puss-puke word. I'll tell you something else: I don't want to see your face near me again, you follow? And if we *do* lose the game, I'll guaran-fucking-tee you it's gonna be *your* face in the crapper, not Stillson's, and I'm gonna be the first one shitting on it!

The fantasy passed, a lightning transition from tavern to hotel room, and I stared at the mirror to see my pale, perspiring face.

If my subsequent laughter was a bit nervous, I nonetheless knew I was making progress. If Etore Wisting was a poor choice, was not Jake Kolacka an excellent one? Indeed, how could I possibly do better than Kolacka?

To make the best use of time, I set Friday as a target date. Friday would be my day of decision. I would not go to sleep on Friday night without having chosen my two colleagues. Nor would I decide on anyone prior to that date. From this vantage point, it seemed to me that the actual fixing of the game should not be done until Saturday—though certainly no later. (I reserved for myself the right to change my mind about that, presumably to schedule these moves a day earlier.) My theory was based on the premise that I would have to hit the right two players on the first swing, so to speak. One strike is out. There could be no vacillating, no compromises, no negotiations. I would arrange my confrontations and lay my offer in whatever way best suited the situation. I believed that on

Saturday, the imminence of the game would be an asset, forcing an immediate, positive response. If a man was of a mind to ponder the offer and weigh the possibilities, I'd have to thrash it out with him then and there. Relying on my persuasive powers, I had to assume I would win such a battle. (I did not care to consider the consequences if I lost.)

Then, too—having agreed to cooperate—the two men would have ample time to consider their own game plans. But not enough time, presumably, to change their minds about it. What's more, the choice of Saturday would prevent any loose talk that extra time has a way of encouraging. With a club such as this one, it was not difficult to imagine one of them dropping an ill-chosen word or two over a beer. And that, of course, would lead to disaster.

I was satisfied with this scheduling. I could only hope I would arrive at the right choices by Friday.

11

Sy Getz was organizing the new locker room set-up when I arrived, working with the Occidental College attendant —a pair of old pros who wasted no words.

"Defense on the left, offense on the right." Sy was directing. He gave me the layout, charted with names and numbers, each player's locker to be designated on a slab of tape marked with his name, their juxtaposition as close to the familiar New York arrangement as possible.

"You're a writer, so write," he said, entrusting me with this grave responsibility while he and assistants went to work unpacking the trunks. As I taped and wrote, the lockers were filled with helmets, pads, shoes. Practice uniforms were hung up, then a mass of impersonal clothing such as T-shirts, socks, supporters, shoelaces, and so on were laid out. Two bags of practice balls were set in the corner beside the electric pump. Boxes of new footballs were secured in the coach's office. The last trunk was checked, then shut again, also to be stored, for it contained the dark purple game uniforms for Sunday.

Outside, there was warm sunshine and soft green grass

and distant palm trees. Forty-odd men in T-shirts and shorts ran around like a bunch of kids in a playground in a free-for-all touch football game keeping two balls in play, unlimited passing, a light workout to break a sweat, "to get the feel of the air," as Coach Seager put it. It was a sight to watch chunky interior linemen, who seldom touched a football during the long season, pretending to be wide receivers using head fakes and stutter steps, trying for nifty one-handed catches while linebackers danced like scrambling quarterbacks before throwing fifty-yard bombs with remarkable accuracy. It was all so chaotic, this swirling of bodies in a nightmarish choreography, I was struck by a sense of oncoming disaster.

"Only winners can laugh like that," came a familiar voice from above me, a clammy hand on my shoulder. It was Bob Benson, TV sports commentator and self-confessed authority on everything.

"How about prisoners on a day off?" I replied.

"These are happy young men on the way to a world's championship," he said.

I had to concede the validity of the mood. I thought of a counter-comment such as "The team that laughs on Monday cries on Sunday," but preferred to deny him the ring of it. I did not particularly like this man though I had to admire his abrasive talent. He had made it big by *appearing* to insult everyone (though always with a smile). It was my belief that he actually *didn't* like anyone—he was far too egocentric to like anyone but himself—but pretended to be the opposite of what he pretended to be. An extremely neat feat, as it were, since his compliments, artfully timed and placed, became all the more appreciated. He gripped my arm firmly as though he were directing me toward some unseen camera in a TV interview. From his majestic height, he kept his hand on a man's shoulder, like a great lord condescending to patronize a vassal, always with simulated equality. He was once described as "a man who changed his name from Bernstein to Benson, wore a hairpiece to conceal his baldness, and told it like it is."

BENSON: Remarkable idea, your picking up dirty jocks and all, Gordon. Surely, you're aware of the history of the athletic supporter. . . .

LITTLEFIELD: No, I don't believe I am.

BENSON: The invaluable contrivance was conceived toward the end of the first century B.C. by a Roman named Gonadius. It seemed that the gladiators would suddenly sustain colossal erections at the most violent moments of truth—one of which, history tells us, was summarily severed by an envious rival—much to the horror of palpitating Roman maidens. It was here that Gonadius, a horse breeder by trade, tailored a mechanism more to contain the erotic than to protect the erogenous. It was forged from cast iron.

LITTLEFIELD: One would think that Leonardo da Vinci might have been involved in its improvement. Something more delicate, no doubt.

BENSON: His patrons, the Medici, unfortunately were uninterested in events of the arena. The Renaissance of culture and the arts, you know. Leonardo was reported to have played around with this matter, but more to *expose* the beauties of man than to protect them.

LITTLEFIELD: I am still in the dark, then.

BENSON: Actually, the modern supporter was invented by the Russians—or so they often claim. The Ukrainian word is *djock*, loosely translated as "ballbearing".

LITTLEFIELD: Fascinating, absolutely fascinating.

BENSON: Yes. (He appeared to like that, releasing my shoulder in order to pat it a few times.) Gordon, let me ask you a serious question.

LITTLEFIELD: I wouldn't think of denying you, Bob.

BENSON: Exactly what are you doing here?

LITTLEFIELD: Well, I was on my way to the Bronx Zoo and took the wrong subway——

BENSON: There's talk you're out to get Lester.

LITTLEFIELD: Why, that's absurd. . . . I love him as a brother——

BENSON: A piece of advice, Gordon: cool it, you're no match for him.

LITTLEFIELD: Let me ask you a serious question, Bob. Is it possible to hide your money under a hairpiece?

BENSON: He'll crucify you, Gordon.

LITTLEFIELD: Perhaps you're right, Bob. After all, it's the holiday season and we all have to love each other.

BENSON: I knew I could get through to you.

Well, it might have been one of the great quickie interviews of all time, two great minds without a single significant thought. Perhaps I might have enlivened it with a bit of my own probing, such as: "I'd like to ask *you*, Harold, since you are such an extremely perspicacious chap: if you wanted to fix the Superbowl—I mean, really put the game in the bag, as they say—how would you go about it?" That sort of thing, done as a serious speculation, might have developed into a fascinating three minutes or so. After all, the opinions of celebrities are always intriguing to fans.

"Well, now, isn't that amazing!" I said aloud, and not without eagerness.

"What? What?" Benson demanded to know.

"I believe someone has just knocked Lester Stillson on his ass!"

It was true, and I'd seen it all. In the middle of the touch football game, Oscar Ayers had thrown a quick flare-out to a burly black linebacker named Jo Jo Abels, a few feet from the sideline, and Abels went barrelling into Stillson, 245 pounds of finely honed muscle, sending the diminutive club owner flying through the air like a well-swatted badminton bird.

Everyone immediately raced to the scene. Photographers snapped shutters with one hand and shoved rivals away with the other. All action stopped as players crowded around to see if the boss were likely to croak. Nat Repple, the trainer, had to claw his way through as the club doctor, Doc Knowland, followed closely behind. Benson kept hollering "Who hit him? Who hit him?" grabbing one player after another. It was here that my journalistic training went to work for me: at a funeral, for example, a good reporter does not gaze at the bier but at the mourners. In this instance, I turned from the prostrate body to the bunch of furtively snickering giants in sweat shirts, in their midst, one Jo Jo Abels, now intermingling with his black buddies, and by God, I saw him shake the hand of Oscar Ayers, the very hand that had passed the football. Indeed, from the congratulatory smiles, it was obvious that this had been a perfectly executed conspiracy. The crime of the century, perhaps. A "murder" designed to seem like an overthrown pass. Had not Oscar been a star quarterback in college? The versatility of professionals was not to be belittled. Since my thoughts always centered around the fix, I could not help but note these two imaginative dissidents with the courage to *do* something. Very interesting indeed. I felt enormously reassured by my acumen. Could Benson be any more intrepid than that?

There was a parting of the crowd as Stillson was carried out on a stretcher. Had there been 70,000 in the stands, there might have been an ovation for the injured hero, but on this day, there was total silence. If he weren't already dead, I speculated, cheers would not kill him.

As it turned out, he was just shaken up a bit, as the commentators like to put it. He was taken to the hospital for X-rays, but the early reports that filtered back to the scene of the crime were disagreeably bland.

It was that old reporter, Joe Weed, who predicted the

outcome. "Abels is doomed," he whispered to me.

"But why?" I played the role of the innocent. "It was just an accident."

"Accident, my ass. Lester runs this organization like the CIA. Whatever happened out there, Lester will know it all."

It would seem that a veteran like Jo Jo Abels would know that and be properly cautious, I suggested—to which Joe Weed responded with a shrug, as if to say, find your own answer to that one.

Joe Weed was right, of course. The players were dressing after practice when the axe fell with unerring accuracy, lopping off the head of Jo Jo Abels.

"Fire him!" came the order from a hospital bed. "And fine that bastard Ayers $500!"

This from a man under sedation.

Abels was stunned. I was, myself, when I learned of his history, that rather stirring black saga so familiar yet so choice. The squalid poverty of childhood on an arid West Texas farm; the eruption of size and strength as a teenager and the sudden rise to prominence as a high school football star; the grinding, competitive, bigoted football mill at a large Texas university where he literally had to fight for an education along with the battering he was there to give and take; the stifling machinelike demands of the pros where he was to be a cog again and nothing but a cog so help him God, to count his blessings and appreciate the opportunity because this was his one and only chance in life, if he failed here what in hell would a nigger such as he do to make a living?

"Here ah come all the way to the Superbowl, from Shit City, Texas, to the top of the globe, then that man takes it away from me!"

Lem Bow, the huge lineman, was sympathetic: "We'll win it, brother. You'll get the full share."

"Shit. . . . It's what he do to a man. He makes everybody

into a piece of shit." He dropped his shoes, unable to continue, ashamed of his tears as though tears were beneath him, but he lowered his great black head into his hands and was wracked by sobs.

Again, I glanced at those few daring to support him, the hallmark of the dissident, and I began to jot down names like an FBI agent at a New Left demonstration: St. Clair, Ayers, Jones, Coll. Even a few whites: Kolacka, Noren, Ace Carter. I found it comforting that this multimillion-dollar organization should be run with the ethos of a low-grade reform school. A reflection of Stillson's soul, no doubt, emitting insidious vibrations that drove men to madness. Like a signal from the gods, then, the resulting chaos played beautifully into my hands. How absolutely perfect that the same repelling qualities that had inspired my scheme in the first place would contribute so greatly to its implementation!

It was, of course, the chaos I hungered for. So much so, in fact, that when I saw the devilish Kolacka again, I could not resist making capital of his rage.

"That fucking Stillson's gonna die in his own shit!"

"I doubt that, Jake. Men like Lester know how to keep a tight bowel."

"I tell you, he's a potential psycho. I've seen dozens of these little Napoleons."

"You talk a lot of theory, Jake . . ." I baited him. "Any writer knows there's no payoff on that."

"Shit. Just wait, baby. . . . I'll kick that fucker's ass!"

As they say out here in Hollywood, you couldn't write it any better.

But it was the accuracy of Joe Weed's information that laid heavily on my thoughts: the Stillson spy. The informer. It was a horrible thing to contemplate.

"And the players know about this?" I asked him.

"No doubt."

"But they don't know *who*?"

He shrugged. "There was a guy a year or so ago, his name was Homer Pate. Remember?"

I remembered something about a black wide receiver who was killed in an automobile accident.

"Wrong," Joe corrected me. "Hit-and-run driver."

"Pate was a snitch?"

"*Somebody* thought so."

The thought of murder on a football team was too heavy for me. The further thought that I would soon be confronting two of their numbers to collaborate on the fix added pungency to my fears. It took no great imagination to envision the consequences if I happened to pick a spy to bribe.

12

Tuesday (Five Days to Go)

The project, as I'd put it, was a continuing exercise in aberration. To the Bulls, it seemed as though the Superbowl were but a backdrop to their neanderthal escapades. The motel pool, for example—a gathering place after morning practice when the sun was high, where lotioned wives lounged and gossiped in bright bikinis, and husbands drank tranquilizing beers before afternoon meetings. Consider, then, the impact of a sudden seepage of a blood-red flow through the filter, spreading gruesomely until the entire pool seemed like the site of a carnage. Or, the next day when, at poolside, one saw the chilling sight of a dozen large snakes of undetermined identity slithering menacingly across the surface. Or, more macabre still, the eerie early morning sight of a nude male corpse floating in the mist—a cadaver, as it turned out, purchased from the county morgue by a few of the more enterprising spirits.

The swimming pool as theater. Fear-filled titillations that turned into laughter. Though no one swam, hundreds came to watch. It was intriguing to note the hotel management's shifting reaction to these appalling breaches of decorum (from near apoplexy to amused indifference) as the Glendale Arms suddenly became nationally known. For a while, there was as much talk about the pool as there was about the coming game, and one wondered what fiendish act might follow.

"They say they're gonna bring TV cameras on twenty-four-hour duty. . . . They gonna shoot it all live."

"Maybe they could get Kling to wrassle an alligator."

"How'd anyone know which one was the 'gator?"

"Well, Kling could wear a jersey with his number on it."

"Yeah, slow motion, instant replay, as Kling eats the damn thing."

"Terrific. Scare hell outta the Cowboys."

"Maybe Kling won't go for it."

"He'll do it . . . all we gotta do is call him chicken."

Ed Mann, the press exec, was having a field day with such talk. The L.A. papers ran a story on the pool showing Kling in trunks and football jersey, a knife in his teeth.

Levity and madness. What they dramatically call the Countdown-to-Superbowl. An irrepressible theme, for the Bulls contributed more than a few demonstrations of wildly irresponsible, even lawless, conduct. So wild, in fact, that neither Stillson nor NFL officials could keep them totally under wraps. For example, Jake Kolacka got smashed in a nudie joint on the Sunset Strip and went after a go-go dancer in the middle of her act. Not without an amusing style, as it turned out, for he appeared on stage nude himself, painted like an Apache warrior, seemingly part of the act, delighting the audience with clowning lifts in a fake adagio dance, so convincing that her protests became useless until he actually screwed her in full view of a shocked but enthusiastic audience. On another night, Lem Bow and Tiny LaTourette were arrested for defecating out of car windows as they drove down Hollywood Boulevard—no simple feat by any standards. Then, too, another trio, this one from the suicide squad, invaded a large party in Beverly Hills dressed as apes, having "borrowed" the costumes from Universal Studios, but overextended the mystery of their visit when they insisted on necking with a few of the best-looking women.

I'd heard reports of other such misadventures. Indeed, the locker and press rooms were bubbling with them, so many, in fact, that I began to doubt their authenticity. True or not, it didn't really matter. The fun was in the telling, the wilder the better, the more appalling, the greater the credence.

Only one man appeared to object: Perry Lee Stover, that biblical buff they called the Deacon.

"The devil hisself walks with this club," he whispered to me in passing, almost as though he were not certain he wished me to hear.

I stopped, thankful that he did too, hungering for an excuse to talk to him. "I don't believe you'd get much of an argument about that," I said.

He stared at me, his small, exceptionally round blue eyes blazing in the center of his cherubic pink face. In an ambience of sin, he needed to speak of religious matters, seeking confirmation for his rectitude.

"They pillory me," he charged. "They speak blasphemous of the Lord to justify their evil. I used to lead the team in daily prayer, but they mocked and defiled my words. *Even before the games,* they refused! There can be no peace for they are all soulmates of Satan."

I allowed that this, too, was true, but I was far more concerned about the nature of *his* morality than theirs.

We talked, sipping tea in a quiet corner. He was an enthusiastic informant of all his pieties though I found his sufferings more to my point. He grew up in southern Oklahoma knowing the pangs of poverty, for his father died of a ruptured appendix, unable to get to a hospital in time because "a nigger had stolen the only truck around." A heritage of bigotry and penuriousness became linked to survival. When, in his early teens, his family moved to a small town near the Texas border, he was introduced to football by the local pastor. Too small, it was arranged for him to wash dishes at a diner in barter for all the food he could eat, and as he grew, he exercised, ran everywhere, lifted homemade weights out of discarded pipes and rocks, did sit-ups, push-ups, isometrics, leg lifts. His progress was remarkable, and under the pastor's tutelage, his devotion to Jesus and football became unshakable. He loved the thud of bodies, and he hit (especially against blacks) with a righteous power as though God Himself were giving him signals.

What seemed strange about Perry Lee was that nothing ever changed with him. Fifteen years had passed since his high school days, but he was the same person. To football and God, he added Home and Family. Prayer and thrift remained the dominant virtues, blasphemy the greatest sin.

Still, at thirty-one, he had learned a few things about the world: that white men cheat and steal and profane the name of Jesus as much as blacks, that his teammates despised him, that Lester Stillson had repeatedly exploited him with lies and broken promises. But what burned him most of all was that there were black rookies who made far more than he did.

Nonetheless, he was not one to protest, preferring to bottle it up, to be salved by prayer and the fury of Sunday contact. He was, then, the ideal offensive interior lineman where self-control (no use of hands) was the dominant prerequisite, where he stood rocklike, blocking out bigger men who slugged and taunted him, "rang his bell," and kneed his groin.

"Ah 'preciate your talking to me this way," he said. "Ah git lonely some."

I could see why he might.

I could also see why I'd certainly keep an eye on him. He was such an oddity, it would be difficult not to.

I did not have to keep an eye on Chuck Noren—he kept an eye on me. For one thing, he had an adjacent room, which abetted the growing intimacy. For another, I appreciated his sociability. (He even played a surprisingly strong game of chess for a lineman.) He was full of stories and anecdotes, all of which he would preface with a quick "here's-one-for-your-book" though much of his material was completely irrelevant. There were more than a few goodies, however, especially about "life in the pit," his phrase for his place of work, as when Stonewall Jackson, wanting Chuck to lead the way into the opposition on a quarterback keep, actually fastened his teeth into Chuck's buttock to spur him to a maximal effort. Or, when he once picked up a fumble and started to run with it, Ace Carter jumped on him, riding piggyback, saying "You carry my ball, you carry me with it!" But mostly, I appreciated his struggle to be level headed in a community of weirdos.

"Chuck, I have the feeling you really belong with a straight club like the Giants."

He laughed. "Every team needs an off-horse, Gordon. Don't you know? Makes everyone else feel safe."

"So far as I can find out, you're the only man on the roster who hasn't served time."

"My uncle is a lawyer, that's why."

"Did he teach you how to play chess?"

"Listen, Gordon . . . don't tell Lester I can beat you. The sonovabitch will fire me for sure!"

Then there was the ubiquitous Jake Kolacka. Rumor had it that it was he who'd somehow sneaked into the Cowboys' dressing room and nailed all of Roger Staubach's shoes to the floor.

"Now, that couldn't have been you, could it, Jake?" I asked.

"Inka dinka doo . . ." he sang.

"Well, what next, Jake?"

"Didn't you hear about how I hypnotized the referee?" He didn't wait for my response, but withdrew a gold pocket watch hanging on a chain, let it sway in front of my eyes like a pendulum, his own eyes pouring into mine.

"Why don't you hypnotize Stillson?" I asked.

He smiled, put the watch away.

"I'll do better than that, Gordon. You'll see."

Then, too, there was Jud Kling. Unlike Noren, not in my plans but very much in my experience. Picture, if you will, the Loch Ness monster in Bermuda shorts, center stage at a press conference, facing a battery of what he liked to refer to as "empty suits."

"Hey, Jud, how do you feel?" came the opening question.

"Bored. The Superbowl is a bore."

"But this is your *first!*"

"I been here five days. It feels like forever."

"Don't you like L.A.?"

"Shithouse of the world."

"I thought all you football players liked this town."

"You must be from L.A."

"If you're so bored, Jud, why don't you quit football?"

"*You* must be from Dallas."

A hundred sportswriters with their ballpoints, scrawling on pads to relay these quips to the hometown fans. Ed Mann stood over them all smiling like a successful used car salesman.

"It seems to me," began a contentious youngster with long hair and a bright pastel-pink sportshirt, for a guy who makes the kind of money you make, I can't feel upset about your boredom."

"Believe me, the last thing I want is to upset the press. But I *am* bored. So are a lot of other guys and it's got nothing to do with money. I hear tell that you guys are bored too, trying to figure out what to write, and come to think of it, a lot of you make as much money as we do. So how does *that* grab you, sonny?"

"I don't want to bore you, Kling," another began. "What comments do you have to make about the firing of Jo Jo Abels?"

Well, there was a popper, all right. Step on a crack, break your mother's back. All pens were primed at the ready position.

Kling took a moment to light up a large cigar, savoring the sense of that first puff as though he were sucking on a sugar tit.

"Old Lester is what you might call a ratfucker. Does that answer your question?"

A dozen voices exploded in spasms of curiosity, obviously hoping to exploit this. After all, Kling's choice of word was hardly printable. Kling, however, adamantly refused to oblige.

"Ratfucker," he repeated.

"What *is* a ratfucker, Jud?"

"A man who fucks rats, dummy." Then he signaled with his cigar that he was through with this. "If you guys wanna talk some football, fire away. If not, I'd like to go upstairs where I can jerk off in peace."

No doubt he would, too, and probably with both hands. This was no ordinary chap, even for a linebacker, and I could not pretend to figure him out. Stories about him were legion. Though he spoke little about himself, others said it for him. Needless to say, I stayed clear of him. What amused me at the press conference was the way he handled the clash, while the writers got their kicks in sassing him, like kids poling a long stick at a caged gorilla.

Jud Kling was now thirty and very much his own man.

Put another in that seat and watch him squirm in a stew of pious cliches.

"All right, Jud," someone picked it up, "let's talk football. How are you preparing to stop the Cowboys' running game. Any special adjustments?"

"What for?"

"What for! They got the best running game in the league."

"They never played against us."

"You don't respect their backs?"

"How come you don't mention their interior line?" Kling asked.

"All right, them, too."

Jud puffed twice and blew a cloud of smoke at them, then finally laid it on. "They won't rush a total of fifty yards all day."

"What!!"

Consternation followed by tumult. A hundred ballpoints went at it as a hundred voices screamed questions, all pretty much the same: by what right did he make such a bold, provocative statement?

"They don't belong in the same ballpark with us," he went on, throwing more fuel on the fire, obviously enjoying all this to the hilt. "I'll say one thing more: they'll be lucky if that Roger even finishes the game." It seemed all the more disrespectful that he didn't say his complete name.

It was a blast, all right. Another violation of the predictable norm. (Don't say anything that can end up on your opponent's bulletin board.) Kling was defying the world. To the press, it was pure gold, for it was only the beginning of a new round of rebuttals and counter-rebuttals that was worth a few more thousand words for their eager readers.

Jud watched, his eyes twinkling through the smoke. He had toyed with them, treating them all to a great big lollipop, a respite from his own boredom, no doubt. After all, how often does a linebacker lead a one-man press conference? And if there were repercussions, even from his teammates, that, too, would amuse him. To know Jud Kling was to understand the word "attack."

My own amusement came from the reporters a few minutes after.

"Cockiness won't win a Superbowl," said one.

"You know something? Those guys are gonna fall on their faces."

"I'll tell you something else: the Cowboys are *really* working!"

And so on and on until the indomitable Joe Weed could not tolerate any more of it.

"Listen to the experts—a bunch of dumb boozers who actually believe their own bullshit. The Bulls are the best. Nobody can beat them. Nobody. Not even the miserable cocksucker who owns them."

"New York, New York, it's a helluva town," sang the man from L.A.

"Yeah, New York," Joe snapped. "The whole country hates the Bulls the way they hate New York. The club is the sordid underbelly of the American psyche. Did you ever stop to think that they have the highest penalty record in NFL history? They're oppressed slaves in rebellion but they do exactly what the slave owner wants. They win!"

For a moment, there was silence, for he had overwhelmed them all.

"Weed, you're crazy."

Joe laughed. "My friend, I'm gonna tell you one last thing: this is a team of destiny. You can't stop them. Never have the sides been so dramatically drawn, the good guys and the bad guys. The way I heard it, the Bulls refused to play in white jerseys, they didn't want to louse up their evil image. It's New York against America, by Jesus, and we're gonna kick the living shit out of you dumb Texas bastards."

Old Joe Weed, the bloody poet of the locker rooms.

"C'mon, I'll buy you a drink," I said.

"I always said there's nothing cheap about you, Gawdon."

We stood at the bar tippling tall glasses of Scotch and soda, and I spoke of my awe at Kling's incredible defiance.

"What defiance," Weed scowled. "It was a routine performance. Didn't you see Ed Mann grinning like he'd just found a sack of gold? Jesus, Gordon, can't you see it's all part of the *shtick*?"

I confessed to ignorance.

"You see Lester screw someone and you think, 'Oh, deah, that chap is mean!' But he takes a bunch of thugs and, because of the way he *is* a S.O.B., he's made them all great."

"The old bit about the end justifying the means?"

"The trouble with you is you see only the facade. Gordon, *they're all in it together!* Lester is a tyrant so they can hate him. They hate him so much, they rebel. They even call him a ratfucker so the press can have a ball. Try to see how beautifully it all fits together. Lester *encourages* it. That's his strength, for Chrissakes. It is also theirs. Can you follow that?"

"The worse, the better . . ." I mused.

He laughed. "Something like that."

"Joe . . . I think you're a frustrated Bob Benson."

"And *you*, sir . . . what keeps *you* going?"

The funny thing was, I really wanted to tell him.

13

I don't believe I have ever met a person, however repulsive, for whom I did not feel a certain compassion when I came to know him—until I met Lester Stillson. It was as though he spent all his talents perfecting new ways to provoke my revulsion. I realize the self-serving nature of such an appraisal—it is always convenient to despise the man one seeks to destroy—but I consider myself sufficiently civilized to rise above such pusillanimity. There were even moments of doubt about the entire project when some show of humanity from him might conceivably have distracted me from its pursuit. But Lester was an endless atrocity, and my week in his presence was a continuing reprise of all those squash-court emotions.

Yet even as I weighed such thoughts, I wondered about myself. Was I, perhaps, overloading my prejudices? Merely to state an awareness that my perspective was self-serving does not preclude the possibility that I might actually be guilty of it. No doubt a psychiatrist would suggest that I was not completely at peace with my purposes—and perhaps I wasn't. I did not pretend at being that resolute or singleminded about anything. Indeed, the way I viewed it, that was the name of Lester's game. No introspection, no doubts, and certainly no guilt. He could contend with all aspects of his life without the slightest qualms of conscience. If he cared what others thought of him, like Machiavelli's prince, he knew it was a lot safer to be feared than loved. His strength lay in his power to intimidate, never conceding defeat even in the most petty confrontations as if winning were a religious experience not to be violated.

He was, in all ways, a small man. I speculated on that, relating it to his size itself. Was the key to his nature nothing more than envy? Envy in place of love. He sought the envy of those whom he himself had always envied. And never was this more apparent than at the party he had arranged to be given in his honor.

Picture, then, a sumptuous Bel Air mansion owned by a motion picture magnate (who was, of course, a football fan) and fifty carefully selected guests from the thousands of top echelon people who had come to Los Angeles for Sunday's great event. A California senator, another from Pennsylvania; corporation executives from the Ford Motor Company, General Foods, Burlington Mills; celebrated attorneys and physicians from New York; motion picture stars and producers; and, distinguished by his absence, the ubiquitous Pete Rozelle. (Lester had carefully arranged to be the only active member of the professional football world.) Quietly, tastefully, weaving through this distinguished gathering were photographers and columnists, all equally celebrated, ostensibly to enjoy the festivities but actually to carry the message to the media, as everyone was fully aware. In the last ten years, I have attended countless parties of varying elegance but, with the possible exception of one or two White House affairs, I would be hard put to recall anything to match this one.

The Great Man saw fit to arrive at his own party with

conspicuous tardiness, rolling up the winding gravel driveway in a chauffeured Rolls Royce, emerging at long last in evening clothes that were flashy even for Los Angeles.

What startled me, however, was the sight of the stunning woman who was his companion. It was Patricia!

For a moment or so, I gasped for breath. How long had she been in L.A.? Why hadn't she called me?

Or, more to the point, why was I making so much of the fact that she hadn't?

I circulated with a fresh drink in hand, determined to avoid any embarrassing confrontations. This was Lester's party, not mine. And Patricia was Lester's wife, not mine.

He was a man of many faces, on this occasion, like a night club performer on opening night, all charged up to his eager audience. They never seemed to tire of him, sitting at his feet like aspiring actors around Sir Laurence Olivier as he recounted the sources of his talent. Of course, it was the Superbowl that intrigued them, just as it was the Superbowl that dominated Lester's entire being.

"There is nothing else that matters to me," he confessed. "Everything else is nothing. If I take this gorgeous creature in my arms, even if I take her to bed, I would be thinking only of Sunday. It is an obsession, my friends, such an obsession I can hardly breathe for the waiting."

Oh, he was dramatic. He sat in the large sofa with the lovely Patricia dutifully beside him, his head thrust out of his collar turtlelike, swivelling from side to side to make contact with us all. He brazenly told a saccharine story of his poverty-stricken childhood in New York, a depression-plagued family without a father, when the undernourished Lester would wait eagerly for Sunday noon when his mother's lover, a fireman, would visit with a bag of food. "Once he was late, I was so hungry I could hardly stand up, I thought I would die if he didn't come," which he described as akin to his anticipation of this coming Sunday, an artful allegory that both highlighted the intensity of his emotion and induced admiration for his resourceful climb to the top. Conveniently, his marriage to an heiress, the source of all his football success, was not mentioned.

"Let's face it, the Superbowl is the *crème de la crème*. No single sporting event or entertainment spectacle can top it. When you stop to think about it, more people will watch this game than *any other event in the history of the world!*"

Well, I don't suppose anyone had thought of it quite that way. He lit a cigar, leaving a moment for his words to settle, and a number of heads nodded appreciatively. And that was all he needed.

"Put it this way: General Dynamics closes a $100,000,000 deal with the Pentagon and maybe it gets a paragraph on page fifty-nine of the *New York Times*. Win the Superbowl, your name is on page one of every newspaper in the country."

Then a stout bubbly gentleman in his late forties finally made himself heard. "Lester, I'm warning you, I've got a group of real estate boys together, and they're tired of building high-rise apartments, tired of fighting the construction unions, tired of battling with politicians . . . a bunch of good old-fashioned sportsmen, and we're getting some money together, we're going to buy a football team, the first franchise available, and we're going to knock your damned New York butt right off the top!"

Laughter, applause, general hubbub, all in good friendly competitive spirit. Lester, of course, loved it.

"You do that, Lew, and I'll kiss *your* butt on national TV."

Someone asked him what he did during the games. Was he nervous? Did he smoke a lot?

"Well, I fidget around. I'm up in the spotter's booth and

usually there's not much room. I smoke cigars, yes, I even drink a few slugs from a flask. Sure, I'm nervous. Then they play the 'Star Spangled Banner' and I sing away all my tension."

A good line, and well received. It was the sort of line that Ed Mann might have given him.

"Then I get busy. Take a lot of pictures with my Polaroid, every defensive formation of the opposition, down by down, and I study them between plays. For example, once I noticed that a rival cornerback had his left foot forward when he was in man-to-man coverage, and his feet were parallel when the defense went into a zone. It took six or seven plays before I was certain, then I phoned it down to Coach Seager."

Intensely: "Oh, what happened then?"

Lightly: "Why, we scored another six, I believe."

More applause, and I thought of all those show business accounts of how Milton Berle used to steal jokes from his competitors and use them as his own. I'd heard Lester's story years ago; I believe it originated with Raymond Berry of the Colts, related to cornerback Yale Lary of the Detroit Lions. That Lester should take credit for the insight of a great professional was disgusting. That I should choose to hold my tongue at such a moment was an indication of his extraordinary power over us all.

Needless to say, he also posed as a genius in acquiring players.

"Now, you take a fine receiver like Coley Barone, you know, the boy who was arrested for child molestation in Houston. All that terrible publicity could easily destroy a man. When I heard they wanted to get rid of him, I immediately sent a scout to his neighborhood, just to nose around a bit. We found out that he was a gutsy kid, running six miles a day, seeing his shrink, he was *trying.* That convinced me, and we picked him, rather cheaply, I might add. The rest is history: you don't get many sexually deviant wide receivers who can put almost a hundred points on the board for you."

Yes, Lester got him cheaply, and paid him cheaply, I might add, but he was quick to advise them all that he was *not* in football for the profit. Money simply did not interest him. Only the thrills, the excitement, the Sunday drama. "It's an art form, my friends. A genuinely creative action. To put a great team on that field is like commanding an army. The problems are endlessly complex. You're the general. You have to know everything that's going on, among your aides as well as your fighting men. When you go into battle, you're actually in it as much as the men in those trenches, you suffer the same way, exult the same way. There's nothing like it, it's the most thrilling thing a man can do. Now that I've finally made it to the Big One, I can tell you, there's *no* way anyone can take this victory away from me!"

They ate it up. An aggregation of millionaire professionals and captains of industry feeding on Lester's pap. He had laid out over $10,000 merely for the privilege of gloating in such elegance. His words were a babble of lies and distortions and self-glorifying rubbish but they emerged as gospel delivered by the pope himself. Even Pat seemed totally supportive, smiling at his duplicities, nodding her head with the enthusiasm of one who was hearing this claptrap for the first time. Oh, I rationalized her attitude readily enough, for she had to allay any possible suspicions. Yet I could not take my eyes from her, pressing for some acknowledgment of my presence, even circulating around the rear of the gathering in hopes of catching her eye from another angle.

She had eyes only for Lester.

"Now, you might have heard, I've invited Gordon Littlefield to spend these Superbowl days with the Bulls. You know that says something about this operation, with a literary man as distinguished as he is. He's not a bad squash player, either, I can tell you. He pretty near beat me. Well, Gordon is writing a book about us, from the inside, which goes to show what an open, democratic organization we are. Now, isn't that so, Gordon?"

It was as if the bad guy suddenly handed the good guy his gun. There was no question but that I could shoot him right then and there. What was he up to? Why was he leaving himself open? Had he set up someone in this room to put me down if I dared to open my mouth? My mind whirred with the possibilities, but in the last analysis, what dominated my decision was the potential death of my project.

"Yes, quite so, Lester."

He smiled, but not with any conspicuous satisfaction. Was he disappointed? No doubt, under the circumstances, I could have rocked a few cradles here, but old Lester would have had the last word, would he not? After all, this was his party. Would a real gentleman insult his host?

I slipped away and poured myself a fresh drink, then walked out to an unlit corner of the spacious garden with its sweet jasmine smell of Bel Air affluence, the sprawling elegance of a live oak silhouetted against a starry sky. I drank my Scotch and breathed deeply of the perfumed air hoping that somehow, in this shank of the evening, Pat would find her way out here to share a glance, a touch of the hand, a smile.

Obviously, she had other ideas.

14

Wednesday (Four Days to Go)

There was a news report on Wednesday that Jo Jo Abels, on being fired, had become drunk and disorderly, ending up in a street fight in which he was so badly thrashed by three men, he'd been sent to the hospital. The news of this abomination circulated through the locker room after practice, adding another layer of resentment toward the callousness of their common enemy. Yet it shocked them not at all, for whatever Lester Stillson had done to Jo Jo was really no different than what he continued to do to them all. Or so they reacted, mumbling like victims so attuned to their own destruction they could hardly be expected to rage at the slaughter of another.

Jake Kolacka, however, was my man of action. When I saw him in the locker room that afternoon, he was pacing the floor in front of his cubicle, back and forth like a bear in a cage. He saw me staring at him as I collected towels, no doubt an added stimulant to his eccentric nature. He came over to the towel bin, his dark eyes sparkling with conspiratorial glitter.

"Gordon, I'm all set!" he muttered, his voice muffled by

his towel as he pretended to dry his face. "I'm going to *kidnap* the sonovabitch!" Then he turned away, not daring to leak another word.

Remembering my little provocation the day before, I was intrigued by his earnestness. Kidnap Lester? Actually kidnap the man? Toward what end? I played around with the thought, then abandoned it, unable to accept its validity.

However, after dinner, he was in my room with a friend of his, a Los Angelino named Dawkins who was dressed in a chauffeur's uniform.

"Oh? We going out formal?" I asked.

"Come as you are," Jake replied.

"Jake, what is this? I mean, I have things to do." (Like sit around waiting for Patricia to call.)

"Believe me," he said, "you'll never do anything that's better." And the two of them grabbed my arms, firmly leading me out.

Dawkins, it seemed, had managed to replace Stillson's regular chauffeur. He would drive Lester to his house way out in Topanga Canyon, near Malibu. A perfect spot for a kidnapping, Kolacka explained; isolated in winter, too far from the highway to be seen or heard. Stillson would be deposited in the bedroom, prevented from escaping by Dawkins' trained German shepherd named Paws, who would sit in the living room.

"Can't Stillson get out through the bedroom window?" I asked.

"Cantilevered over a seventy-foot drop?" Kolacka smiled.

But the *pièce de résistance*, Kolacka explained, was that Dawkins, who worked for the phone company, was rigging up a special phone connection to a neighbor's house. Stillson would be able to use the bedroom phone, but all calls would go through this hookup.

I confessed only to skepticism, never believing for a

minute that any of this would happen, nor even that Kolacka was serious. Only when I found myself driving along the snakelike road over the Santa Monica Mountains into Topanga did I realize the true intensity of this madman. And when I saw Lester's rented Rolls Royce twisting into a narrow dirt driveway up to a distant cantilevered house, I began to prepare myself for the adventure.

We settled into the neighbors' house, an obliging couple named Rose and Charley, and drank beer until Dawkins himself arrived in the Rolls. Kolacka, I noted, took command of the operation with competence and style. Not only was he going to pull this off, he was going to enjoy it to the fullest.

"Just a question of time before he picks up that phone!" he said. For this eventuality, he and Dawkins had devised an audio-visual set-up wherein the action would be played out in front of us all, every word tape-recorded on a gadget activated by the phone itself. A telephone drama, as it were. I had but to imagine Lester's frustration in that isolated bedroom with a snarling German shepherd just beyond his door.

"He's probably hollering for help out the bedroom window," Kolacka speculated, and we all fell silent, holding our breath on the somewhat ludicrous assumption that we might be able to hear him.

Then, finally, a light flashed on the electronic device beside the phone.

"Yeeeah!" Kolacka shouted in boyish eagerness.

The digital panel below registered the "O," that Lester had dialed, and Rose picked up her phone, using a cheerful professional voice, saying, "Operator . . ."

Immediately, Stillson's voice came over the speaker, his fury bubbling with every word.

"Get me the damn police! Emergency!" he snapped.

"Yes, sir," said Rose, and handed the phone to the grinning Kolacka as Dawkins triggered the familiar telephonic sound of a new connection.

"Sgt. Pissmeyer, Los Angeles Police..." sing-sang Kolacka in true camp, assuming the lisping manner of a blatant homosexual.

"Sergeant, this is Lester Stillson, owner of the New York Bulls. I've been kidnapped!"

"Oh, my..."

"For Chrissakes, come get me outta here!"

"You mean to say, Mr. Stillman, your kidnappers permitted you to call the police?"

"There's no one here. Just a dog."

"You've been kidnapped by a *dog*?"

"Dammit, Sergeant, I'm up here above a canyon!"

"Which canyon, Mr. Pillman?"

"How the hell do I know! Can't you trace the phone?"

"What's your number, please?"

"452–4331."

"Hold on, Mr. Pillbox."

Kolacka pushed the hold button and came up laughing.

"Beautiful!" he said, taking a healthy drink from his can of beer. He winked at me, then returned to the phone.

"Mr. Sillyman, you are calling from Sodom's Tavern in West Los Angeles."

"What! That's impossible. This is no goddam tavern. 452–4331. Check it again!"

"Mister, I think you've had a few too many!" then hung up on him.

Light out, followed by an outburst of laughter.

And, of course, the light went right back on again.

"Operator, can you check the number I'm calling from?"

"452–4331, sir."

From here, Stillson changed to "411."

"Information, what town please?" asked a new voice from Rose.

"Sodom's Tavern in West L.A."

"One moment, please." Pause. "Sir, that's 452–4331."

"Christ!"

Light out.

"It's only the beginning," Kolacka grinned, then nodded to Dawkins. "Ring him, pal," he said.

A few seconds later, the light went back on.

"Yes?" came Stillson's eager voice.

"Is Sam Sodom there?" Kolacka now spoke in the thick slurring tones of a far-gone drunk.

"Who?"

"Ain't this Sodom's Tavern?" He even added a hiccup.

"Who is this?"

"Gus Gommorah. Where's old Sam?"

"Listen Gus . . . I'm in trouble. I'm Lester Stillson, owner of the New York Bulls. I've been——"

"I don't give a shit if you wuz King Kong. Put Sam on."

"Gus, listen to me, I'm a rich man. . . . I'll make it worth your while."

"You're so rich, whattaya doing in a dump like Sodom's?"

"What are you talking about! This is not Sodom's. This is not a tavern! I've been kidnapped!"

Quietly, "Mister, I think you need a drink."

Light off, and a fresh burst of Kolacka laughter.

"Couldn't be better," he said.

I had to admit, this was extraordinary.

"Like I said, Gordon, I'm going to drive him nuts!" Kolacka went on. "Stark, raving nuts!" The prospects were intriguing, all right, especially when Stillson called the Glendale Arms, whereupon Rose immediately became the hotel switchboard operator.

"Glendale Arms, good evening."

"Get me Ed Mann," barked Stillson.

Using the other phone, Dawkins made that connection, and when Ed got on the line, Dawkins shifted the call to the prank phone.

"Ed!" came Stillson's overjoyed voice.

"Yes, Mr. Stillson. Where are you?"

"I'm trapped in the hills . . . kidnapped, I swear. I don't even know where. Something to do with Sodom's Tavern, and there's no one here but a vicious dog."

"Did you call the police?"

"Ed, listen, I don't like the feel of this. Get hold of the police, find out where I am. The number is 452-4331. Ed, this is a bitch!"

"The police. Right."

Light off.

Kolacka danced around the room like a kid at his birthday party. "He's ripe, I tell you. He's gonna fall apart!" His eyes seemed to bulge with his anticipated triumph, threatening to pop right out of their sockets. "I've got him! I've got him!" he roared, and he leaped toward the window, lifting the frame from the sash with such power it almost broke apart. Then he canted his head toward the distant hill and bellowed into the gathering twilight: "FUCK YOU, LESTER!"

When he pulled back into the room, he was calm again, quietly lowering the window, chuckling slyly, amused at the child in himself that could make merriment out of all this. Having extended his passions, he sat with a fresh can of beer as though he were in the locker room after a successful game.

Waiting now, that was the beauty part. Kolacka reveled in the waiting. "We should've rigged up a mike over there," he said to Dawkins. "Maybe even a hidden TV camera."

Finally, the light on the panel went on, then the digits calling the Glendale Arms. Rose went to work, and once again, the connection was made with Ed Mann.

"Mr. Stillson, I've been trying to reach you!"
"Well, what happened! What'd you find out?"
"This is crazy, but there is no Sodom's Tavern."
"What!"
"No, sir. And there's no listing for your number. The phone company insists that there's no such number."
"There's got to be. We're talking, ain't we!"
Silence for a beat.
"Mr. Stillson, I spoke with Captain Rafferty of the L.A. Police. *He* checked with the phone company. He can't make head or tail of this. . . ."
"What am I supposed to do!"
"I don't know, Mr. Stillson."
"Christ, who the hell could be doing this to me!"
"Captain Rafferty asked me that. He wanted to know who it was who brought you there."
"What's the damn difference! Look, Ed, what's Rafferty's number?"
"725-1000."
"I'll get back to you."
Light off. Light on. Then the digits of the L.A. Police Department. Kolacka grabbed the phone with the eagerness of a long-lost lover. And when he spoke this time, his voice was slow, in a fine, thick Irish brogue.
"This is Captain Rafferty."
"Lester Stillson, Captain."
"Who?"
"Lester Stillson, owner of the New York Bulls. Ed Mann just talked to you."
"Ed Mann? Never heard of him."
"What! He just gave me your number. He said——"
"He's lying. I've been talking to my bookie for twenty minutes."
"Captain. You are Captain Rafferty?"
"Are you suggestin' that I'm not?"
"No sir. Captain, please . . . listen carefully. . . ."

"Don't give me orders, mister. Nobody gives the captain orders—except the mayor."

"I'm sorry. It's just that I'm in trouble."

"You're the owner of the Bulls, you say?"

"That's right. Stillson, Lester——"

"Stillson, yeah. I hear you're supposed to be a real prick."

"Listen——"

"Yeah, a cheap sonovabitch who'd sell his mother to a syphilitic pimp."

"Captain!"

"I see slime like you every day in this job. Mean cocksuckers who don't deserve to live."

"Please, Captain. I need help!"

"All right, I'll help you. I'll give you a tip. I'm an old football player myself, so I know. You throw short to your backs circling out of the backfield. Throw to your tight end, eat away at them with short stuff, you do that and you'll win. And one more thing——"

"Jesus Christ, *will you listen to me!*"

"Take it easy, buddy, it's only a game."

"*I've been kidnapped!*"

"You've got no cause to yell at me. I don't favor that!"

"Captain, please . . ." And finally, there it was, the first time I ever heard Lester Stillson beg for anything. "Please . . . I don't understand this. Captain, I'm afraid. Please . . ."

"That's more like it, mister. I suggest you take it easy for the night. Things'll look better in the morning. G'night."

"*Captain!*"

But Kolacka hung up, exhausted with his victory. "Enough . . . enough," he gasped, his face red and sweated. "You're a genius," he said to Dawkins, then removed the cassette from the tape machine.

So it was that the show was over. Having broken his man, Kolacka had had enough. Dawkins would call off his dog in an hour or so, leaving Stillson the freedom to leave. It was less than a mile to the road were the Rolls would be waiting for him.

"Well, how did you like that, old buddy?" Jake was glowing like a Christmas tree.

It was no ordinary feat, I had to admit, but my calculated guess was that he was underestimating his victim.

"Lester doesn't crumble so easily," I warned him.

"Bullshit. He's a piece of cake."

I laughed at Kolacka's insolence. He was like a smart little brat who hadn't learned how to lose. In this setting, that was fine with me. Kolacka was my main concern, not Stillson, rapidly emerging as the epitome of all my anticipated triumphs. It was as if God Himself had created this man for my purposes, then blessed me with the acumen to expoit him. Because of Kolacka, the entire experience was becoming more stirring than I'd ever imagined it could be. I had never felt so alive, so involved in what I was doing, as though everything that had gone before in my life was rendered pale by the intensity of this week's drama. My nerve endings were so alive, I was ready to pop the big question right then and there. Why not? Wasn't this a superbly engineered moment to be properly seized? Was there any doubt but that this man was the ideal choice for the fix?

"Jake . . ." I said. "I'd like to talk to you about a totally different matter."

He picked up on it immediately. "I know. You want to write a book just about me."

What amazed me was my immediate relief, for almost as I'd spoken those loaded words, I'd sensed that I was terribly premature.

"Right. I'd call it *Jake the Jock.*"

"Inka dinka doo . . ." he sang.

He laughed, and I took a deep breath to relax, suddenly remembering another such moment when I'd made the mistake of impetuousness. It was, of course, the one time when I'd asked a lady to marry me. Another perfect setting, to be sure, a soft summer night walking on a Southampton beach, the surf sparkled silvery bright under an exceptionally round moon, an overwhelming romantic wash of emotions, all very idyllic. She'd accepted me, and for an hour or so, I'd fantasized on the majesty of it all. It was less so in the morning, of course. I supposed that the best setting for such vital decisions is rather a stifling traffic jam. In fact, it was precisely there, some weeks later, that we decided to cancel the entire arrangement. And though I spared myself a disastrous marriage, I nonetheless lost a most agreeable paramour.

I was pleased, now, that I'd held my tongue. I would stick to my schedule. I would use the next two days to make certain this would be a perfect marriage.

15

I stopped at the Arms Tavern for a tranquilizing beer, wondering what new flapdoodles awaited me. I saw, instead, the slumping, depressed head of my square friend, Chuck Noren.

He was alone and absolutely still, his hand wrapped around a beer bottle as though he were preparing to use it as a weapon. I watched him for a few seconds, wondering what was going on in that constantly bewildered head of his.

"You planning on spending the night here?" I asked him. "Isn't there curfew?"

"Fuck him."

"Fuck who?"

"Stillson."

"What happened now?" I asked. I had a very special penchant for conversations that began this way.

"Fuck him on general principles," he scowled.

"Writers always prefer details."

"Bartender, two more!" he cried out.

"You'll miss bedcheck," I offered.

"Fuck him and his bedcheck."

Well, that, too, was all right with me. I accepted the beer, though I had no intention of drinking any more of it.

"He called me in today. . . . He says, 'Noren, I'm not satisfied with your attitude.' I says, 'What's wrong with my attitude that ain't wrong with *every*body's attitude?' He says, 'Noren, you're the center of the goddam line. You're the key man. I expect you to be an inspiration to the others. You know what you are? You're an inspiration for shit!' "

He drank a glass of beer as though it were his first after a long hot practice. From the bleary look of his eyes, the soft curl of his mouth, he must have already downed a dozen.

"You know what he did? He 'relieved' me of my bonus, the bonus he promised me if we won the pennant."

Interesting how my exhilaration had a way of rising in direct proportion to the sinking of his hopes.

"That's a damned shame," I said.

"Three thousand dollars!" And he banged his glass on the formica top, snapping it. It cut his hand, but he didn't care. In seconds, the blood was oozing from it, but he still didn't care.

"Would you believe it? He was grinning . . . I mean, *really* grinning!"

I said nothing. I was so pleased, I was afraid to speak. I drank some beer instead.

"Let's go out and get drunk, Gordon."

I looked at him, wondering if I should try to stop him, to put him to bed, somehow. I decided to go with him, not because of my selfish needs, but because I could see the extent of his own. He was going out no matter what.

"Come on, Mr. Inspiration. I'll buy the first few rounds," I said.

He smiled through his depression. "A friend, by Christ, a friend!"

I took him to a watering place on Ventura Boulevard where we shifted from beer to Scotch. He drank the Scotch, but added a bottle of beer as a chaser. His capacity was staggering, and the more he drank, the more he talked.

He told me about his wife, Lillie, and how much he missed her. She hated the football world, though, and especially Lester Stillson. He missed his two little girls (he showed me pictures), but Lillie refused to stay in New York with him. His home was outside of Asheville, North Carolina, where he had grown up. His father owned a gas station. Chuck still worked there in the off season, ran the service department. He hated it. Nothing ever worked out for him, he insisted, but he loved his wife, he kept repeating that, and he loved his two little girls.

I got him home around four o'clock in the morning.

"You're a terrific fella, Gordon. You're gonna write a helluva damn book, all right. You'll see. Terrific fella . . ."

In light of the vital services I might soon be asking him to perform, I found such adoration, even when smashed, highly encouraging.

The only thing that bothered me was that there were no messages from Pat.

16

Thursday (Three Days to Go)

There was a pervasive sullenness to the Bulls on Thursday morning, very much in keeping with the grey murkiness that hung over the Los Angeles basin. I had seen the depth of this mood for days. For all the laughter, there had been little joy. They made jokes because that was their style. Jokes had little to do with their feelings; they were more a conditional response to the drudgery of the day than any manifestation of pleasure. I supposed, after six long months, they'd been at it too long, and that this final week of practice and public relations had turned into a tedious farce.

Sunday, it seemed, was too long in coming.

I sat at breakfast, picking up the scattered dialogues of this table and that. The talk, it seemed, was concentrated on the sports pages of the L.A. *Times* wherein it was reported that the Cowboys were furious at Jud Kling's contempt.

" 'The locker room bristled as they spoke of it,' " Oscar Ayers was reading. " 'Fifty yards! Fifty yards!' they cried out, unable to believe such blasphemy!' "

"Them dumb newspaper people. They'd kill your old lady just to take a picture of you crying at the grave."

"Yeah, it's always lets-you-and-him fight."

"How do you get even with a writer, anyway?"

"Tell 'em lies."

"Like what?"

"Like 'The Bulls are the most overrated team in football.' "

"That ain't a lie."

"Now this here bacon is the most overrated bacon I ever ate," said big tackle Lem Bow, lifting a long soggy slice dripping with fat. "You figure a pig would be proud to end up like that?"

"Pigs are like football players. They got no pride."

"I swear, this is the same damn fried egg I throw'd in the garbage yesterday."

"How'd you know that?"

"You can see where the cook spit on it."

"Shit, man, that's what gives it vitamins."

"Hey, Lem, what'd you guys do last night?"

"Oh, man, we had a ball. Went to this big party with a lot of Hollywood starlets, lots of fine wine and good grass, danced until 3 A.M., then got sucked and fucked and just managed to get back here in time for all this fine grub."

"Yessir . . . old Willie and me were going to stop in there, but Lester himself took us to a really posh pad. . . . I mean, champagne and caviar, the works. Ain't that right, Willie?"

"Right as rain."

"Shee-it, the goddam coffee ain't hot."

"Man, what day is this?"

"Ain't that a shitfuck? I was just wondering about that."

"We ain't *never* gonna play this football game, you know?"

"What football game? We here to play a football game?"

"Yeah, man, ain't you heard? They gonna have linesmen, referees, everything."

"Referees . . . shee-it. We once played a game without them motherfuckers . . . in high school. They never showed, so we played anyway. And you know something? It weren't bad at all. I mean, we just played clean because of it."

"That's 'cause you didn't know no better."

"Hey, lookee here: ain't this a cockroach in my coffee!"

"No, man that's a coffee bean."

"How come it got legs?"

"Coffee beans got legs. How else they gonna get here from Brazil? Ain't that right, writer?"

"Some say legs, others say wings. Perhaps it depends on which part of Brazil they come from."

"Why don't you ask the cook, Lem?"

Lem thought about it for a moment, nodded, then left with his coffee cup.

"It says here that there's a chance it's going to rain on Sunday. The writer says that'll help the Cowboys because they run very fine mud plays. It says that Bob Newhouse has an outboard motor up his ass and he's gonna squish for big yardage."

"The writer say where he gonna get the fuel?"

"All he gotta do is keep farting to the goal line."

"Man, he fart that much, no one'll tackle him nohow."

"The writer tells 'bout that. He says Newhouse has gone on a special fart-making diet. Lots of beans. It says here he gets special beans imported from Mexico."

"That's *jumping* beans."

"Well, that's so he can fart and jump at the same time."

"Suppose he shits by mistake?"

"That's a fifteen-yard penalty."

"The writer say that?"

"Yup. Says it's rule number thirty-eight, paragraph 3A, 'unnecessary roughage.' "

"Wow. What's the ref's hand signal on that?"

"He pulls down his pants."

"I thought that was the signal for buggery."

"Only when he bends over."

"Man, I sure hope it rains hard."

"No, it never rains out here in January. The writer himself says that."

"I dig that writer. He's got all the facts. What's his name anyway?"

"Milton Motherfucker."

"Hey, Gawdon, ain't that your pen name?"

"I don't have a pen name."

"That's the trouble with you; no real class."

Lem returned from the kitchen and sat down again, still staring into his coffee cup.

"He gave me another coffee bean. He said, if you watch real close, they'll fuck, and then you can have a coffee tree."

"This sure is a fine hotel. Gonna bring my old mother and father out here for a vacation some day."

"We ain't *never* gonna get outta here, Oscar. This is *it*."

"Man, I had that dream *twice* already!"

Then, suddenly, the dialogue dissolved and all heads bent low, forks scraping final bits of food off plates long since abandoned. I had been here long enough to know the cue: Stillson was approaching.

I sipped tepid coffee and pretended to jot down some notes, yet I felt his presence behind me. What I never would have anticipated, however, were the two ostensibly friendly hands that rested on my shoulders.

"G'morning, boys. Everybody okay?" He was all very bright and cheerful, not like a man who'd been kidnapped the night before.

"Yes, suh!" came the sullen reply.

"And how're *you* doing, Gordon? I hope you men are giving him all the help you can."

"Oh, yes, suh!"

"I told him that you would, you know. I don't know a writer anywhere whom I'd rather have with us. I'm really looking forward to reading his book." Then, as though to put the icing on the cake, "Stop by later, Gordon. We ought to spend more time together, don't you think?"

A man of consummate guile, one could say. An artist at picking his spots. How better to compromise my standing with these men than for him to suggest friendship and intimacy with me!

The effect was instantly apparent.

"Huhn!" came the smug triumphant snarl of my black nemesis, Henry Coll, and a dozen suspicious glances suddenly floated my way.

Practice that morning was a lot like breakfast. It was as if the players had gorged themselves on resentment and the resulting bile was befouling their mood. They turned their hatred of Stillson into a hostility toward each other, toward themselves, even. During the first few minutes running pass routes, wide receiver Gil Warner slowed down as he made his cut, then stopped completely. He told the coach he felt a muscle pull coming on. He didn't want to run any more.

Stonewall Jackson overthrew the next four passes. Ted Monnell was equally off target.

When they ran running plays, simple handoffs were fumbled on three successive plays. Z, for example, dropped one, picked it up, angrily kicked it out of the park.

Gino Baletti, an offensive tackle, picked himself up after mild confrontations with the defensive front four, walked to the sidelines, and threw up.

The defensive line, practicing tackle-end stunting, a familiar ploy to circumvent blockers on a blitz, bumped heavily into each other and fell down screaming at each other.

At 10:25, Coach Seager decided to end this comedy of errors, but Stillson would have none of it. If the club could not practice properly they would have to run, and he ordered them to take eight hard laps around the track. Nobody would go inside until the two hours had expired. Nobody cared.

The afternoon practice was no better than the morning. Coach Seager's voice was pitched several notches higher than usual as if stridency would motivate where all else failed. Predictably, it moved no one. An entire squad that did not want to practice—like a writer blocked from any capacity to put sensible words on paper. They clowned as they ran pass routes, for example, moving downfield in slow-motion imitations of TV instant replay as the defensive backs backpedaled in comparable style. Then, stopping, reversing directions like a projector turning backwards, an art they'd cultivated to a remarkable balletlike efficiency. The punter actually kicked a football backwards, over his head, then fell down laughing. Carter took a handoff from Jackson and ran sixty yards—the wrong way. Huddles turned into travesties as everyone talked at once.

Then, for no apparent reason, tight end Willie Jones suddenly tore into Chuck Noren, fists swinging maniacally in body blows as the two giant padded bodies went grappling to earth in what seemed like a savage intent to kill. I watched in horror while others watched in glee, like spectators at the Friday night fights, not caring that one or both might get hurt so close to game day. Even Kling seemed indifferent, opting for a drink of Gatorade on the sidelines, then sat on the bench as though this were an excuse for a time-out. Minutes passed before the battlers expended themselves and drew apart, breathing heavily, glaring at each other in a bewildering frustration.

Stillson was there through it all, screaming like a stuck pig, and when Coach Seager called a two-minute water break, Lester raced to the sidelines ahead of them, his face red with a hunger for vengeance. I was standing by the Gatorade when he passed me, slamming awkwardly into the loaded table, scattering and spilling everything in a fury.

"No!" he shouted. "I say, no one drinks!"

Then he stood in front of the mess, arms spread out as though that, too, were necessary to stop anyone who tried. The players stopped, staring at the spilled cool liquid while muttering predictable obscenities.

"This is a practice, not a goddam vacation!" Lester ranted on. "Now, get back there and go to work!"

They returned to the playing field, making a joke of their need for water, clutching their throats like parched Arabs stumbling across the desert. Nor was the practice any better for the punishment, eventually driving Lester off the field in frustration. And a few minutes later, when Seager finally ended the disaster, they let out a cry of triumph, lifted him to their shoulders and carried him off the field.

It was hard to decide who had won the day.

I found Willie Jones sitting in his locker stall, his black head lowered, towel draped over his shoulders. He was so still, I thought he might be asleep.

"What happened out there, Willie?" I asked.

He was a gentle type, or so I'd found him, too shy to speak unless spoken to. He did not look up but merely shook his head.

"You went at Chuck like a wildcat," I persisted. "Why?"

He shrugged, embarrassed at his own evasiveness.

"I dunno," he said finally.

"Did he bait you? Did he say anything to you?"

No response.

His large brown eyes were as pathetically vacuous as those of a dog who'd been castigated for he knew not what. The message was clear enough: he was not about to talk to me, not about the incident, not about anything. Because of those two slimy hands on my shoulders?

I left him, speculating on how long this silly freeze would last. I was interested in this man and I wanted to see if his thick skull could be penetrated. For my purposes, stupidity was not necessarily objectionable; if Willie was smart enough to be a cog in a winning machine, how much intellect was needed to be a proverbial monkey wrench?

Later, I asked Noren about the incident, wondering, now, if he too were going to be hostile. He was merely diffident. "Willie's a dumb nigger prick. There's no 'counting for what a dumb nigger prick might do. You look at him once too often, he blows up. Come to think of it, he blows up a lot."

The volcano theory. An unstoppable force that suddenly erupts for inexplicable reasons.

To learn about Willie, one does not go to Willie. Certainly not as a primary source. The trouble was, no one appeared to know him very well. He was so lacking in personality, he seemed without texture. A thickly muscled phantom, perhaps.

Curious, for he'd been a starting tight end for five years. Another black conversion, I learned. He'd been a 235-pound fullback at Grambling College, a star who would crash into the line with knees high (and, it was said, eyes closed), totally oblivious to blocks or holes or what they call "daylight," but with highly impressive statistics. What's more, he had great hands, huge grasping frankfurter-sized fingers that wrapped around a football the way an average man might hold a banana. As Ed Mann once put it, "He was the perfect tight end if he could be taught to block." Apparently he was, though there were no stats on that.

Willie had come from backwoods farm country outside of Moultrie, Georgia, the youngest of nine children. His father was huge, even bigger than Willie. An entire family of giant bodies and pea brains. Nor did Willie have the benefit of adequate schooling. He never even saw Moultrie until he was fifteen, when he first played football, nor any city of size until he was sent to Grambling.

It was the barest bones of a background, but better than none at all. Few knew if he had married. He would hang around at times, disappear at others. No one knew, or cared, where he went. He never spoke to anyone during the games nor anyone to him, even when he made a great catch and plowed for a vital first down.

"Willie is an enigma wrapped in an animal," Ed Mann had once said in a whimsical paraphrase of Winston Churchill's remark about Stalin's Russia.

Then, later that day, I bumped into him in the lobby.

"How goes it, Willie?" I asked, more as a greeting than a question.

I was happy to see he was no longer hostile.

"Ah goes OK, but the world goes KO."

It stopped me; this twisting of letters into counterpoint seemed highly original.

"How so?"

"Well, ol' Jo Jo . . . he in bad shape."

"I heard he'd gotten drunk."

"You hear with the wrong ear, mistuh."

"Well, what *did* happen, Willie?"

He stopped to consider his answer, staring at me with those quizzical eyes, then his face assumed a cold sardonic grin. "Why don't you check him out, Mistuh G? Like you done check *me* out?"

More of an enigma, infinitely less of an animal.

As a result of the wasted practice day, Stillson sought to punish them all by calling another evening of meetings: a replay of films, more board talks, a review of match-ups. The works. Anticipating rebellion, I was amazed to see that they hardly batted an eye.

"What's going on?" I asked Rolland St. Clair when back at the Arms. "You guys going to tunnel out of here at midnight and make a break for the border?"

"Nobody's talking to nobody," he replied.

"I'll buy you a beer," I said.

"I need a screw not a brew."

"I daresay one is not necessarily exclusive of the other."

He scowled with mock contempt. "You talk like Bob Benson."

In the bar, he relaxed. The very sight of a glass of beer seemed to sedate him.

I liked this man for the manner with which he handled his coolness. Too many blacks spent their energies imitating the Walt Frazier style, but Rollie had no need to imitate anyone. He was genuinely beautiful, with or without sartorial splendor. He seemed thoroughly indifferent to the clothes he wore. Nor did he wear Borsalino hats, flashy capes, or platform shoes. Without pomp, Rollie was his own man. It was his beauty he flashed, and I suspected it was all that really mattered to him.

For it all, I had considered him a likely prospect, largely, I supposed, because he liked me. Or, perhaps more accurately, he admired my own style. Nor was he above finding allies among selected celebrated honkies such as myself for whatever benefits such contacts might lead to. It suggested a willingness to trust my judgments.

"Yeah, man, it's tired time, all right," he said.

"The calm before the storm?"

"Somethin' like that."

"Is that typical with ballplayers?" I asked.

"With this outfit, who knows?"

"Saving themselves for Sunday?"

"Football is a Sunday game, man. This weekday shit's a drag."

"Aren't you supposed to be making sure of assignments, getting all those defensive keys down pat?"

"Sheeeit, my man goes thattaway, I go thattaway. Big deal. . . . Man, I could play for them Cowboys on Sunday and do just as good a job. It's reflex and experience. The rest is jazz."

"Don't the films help?"

"I don't need to watch 'em no more."

We paused for another beer.

"What're you going to do when the season ends, Rollie?"

"Well, I been thinking about the films, you know. OJ says he can set it up for me. We win that Superbowl, I just might stick around here to give it a shot."

Interesting, the way a chill coursed through me. The movies, the movies. His words were like a cloud passing in front of the sun. The man wanted to be in the movies, and for all his cool, I could taste his intensity. I remembered seeing him on televised games, jogging off the field after making a crucial third-down tackle, his helmet in hand as cameras persistently zoomed in tight to show how pretty he was. Would a man with such vanity lend himself to my rather dubious project?

Immediately, I removed him from my mental list of prospects—as when a woman you're pursuing suddenly tells you she's in love with another man.

"I wish you luck, Rollie," I said.

"The name of the fucking game," he nodded.

I was crossing the lobby when Ed Mann caught up with me. Stillson, it seemed, *really* wanted to talk to me. A matter of great urgency, he added. I followed him to the elevator, more apprehensive than I cared to admit to myself. I had never been free of fear that such a man might somehow find me out.

He was stalking the walls of his room like a lion in a zoo, fuming incoherently at his plight. I was relieved to discover that his concern was over the Kolacka Kidnapping and not the Littlefield Fix. I could follow his story of the first affair in the canyon, but a more recent confrontation made no sense. It took a more cogent explanation from Ed to straighten me out.

Apparently, the mayor of Los Angeles had called Lester, accusing him of "insulting Captain Rafferty of the L.A. Police Department, and making up a preposterous yarn about a kidnapping from a tavern that didn't exist, from a telephone number that didn't exist!" As a result, the mayor wanted a letter of retraction, copies to be sent to all Los Angeles papers and TV stations, plus a $5000 check to the L.A. Hospital Fund.

"We were hoping, Gordon, that since you know important people, you could straighten out this ridiculous matter."

The Amazing Jake Kolacka had struck again! He was definitely a "oner" as they identify crazies in crossword puzzles, so uncanny, so wily, so shrewd that I found myself nursing an eerie suspicion that he, not Stillson, might actually be on to my ploy. Though I rejected this immediately—already well aware of the paranoia that lurks in the criminal mind—my respect for the man was unlimited.

"Well, I don't know, Ed. I mean, this is not my town, you know. . . ."

"But can't you find a link? Isn't there someone in New York you can call?"

"I really don't think so."

It was such an obvious cat-and-mouse game, inevitably Lester would have to blast it away.

"Goddammit, Littlefield, let's cut the bullshit!" he hollered. "Just what do you know about this?" and he glared at me with the zeal of a well-informed prosecutor.

It took me back some. How much did he actually know of my involvement? Who could have told him what?

I opted for bland innocence. "Why, absolutely nothing."

"Is that so?" he snickered, convinced I was lying. "Well, one way or another, *you're* gonna fix this mess up! I don't even want to think about it again. You fix it up or *you're out of here*! You got that? No more free ride with this outfit. No more book. Out! And I'm talking about *tonight*!"

At that moment, it seemed absolutely certain that he meant what he said. Nor was this dictum a purely impetuous act, however suddenly and stridently delivered. What intrigued me was the instant realignment of my own perspectives. Whatever Lester did, I found myself prepared to counter it. I began turning over the alternatives with startling clarity when one considers the circumstances.

For openers, I saw how simple it would be to promise that I'd take care of everything. After all, there was really nothing to take care of. All I had to do was call him in a few minutes and tell him that the entire situation had been cleaned up—which left me with the status quo: I would have relieved Lester of his distress but made no progress in my own cause.

It was here that another possibility flashed across my mind: if I had, in fact, provoked Kolacka to enrage Stillson in the first place, could I not now provoke Stillson to enrage Kolacka?

If so, would not Kolacka then be ideally set up for the fix itself?

"Lester, did you ever consider the possibility that the whole kidnapping thing was, quite simply, a hoax?"

"Why don't you check it out?" I suggested. "Call the mayor's office. Find out if he really called you."

He could hardly contain himself. To be insulted was one thing. To be played for a fool was quite another. He grabbed the phone as though he were wringing a chicken's neck, and inside of a minute he had his answer: the mayor hadn't called, couldn't have called; he was out of town and wouldn't be back until Monday.

Then he slammed the receiver back in its cradle so hard it bounded off, trembling momentarily on the floor like a dying black rat.

"All right, Littlefield, let's hear it!"

"There's not much, really. A few snatches of conversation . . ."

"Goddammit, *who was it*!"

Well, there it was. I'd brought it down to the wire. I hesitated only for an instant, and then, with the guts of a burglar blowing a safe, I plunged right in.

"I believe Jake Kolacka was involved," I said.

17

If this ploy seemed somewhat devious, I did not believe for a minute that I was putting Kolacka in any jeopardy. Stillson would never fire a linebacker like Jake just before the Superbowl. Jo Jo Abels, on the other hand, was backed up by Etore Wisting and was expendable. Kolacka was not. Stillson would never sacrifice victory for retribution. He would find a way to punish him. Indeed, I counted on that. A fine, perhaps, or a restriction. Some insidious form of humiliation. Whatever, it would enrage Kolacka, and *that* would be *my* reward.

By the time I got back to my room, I sensed only the intoxicating kick of anticipated success. There was no question but that I had done my work well. Though I had a full day left on my timetable, for all intents and purposes I had made my decisions. Beautiful choices, so artfully formed and nurtured in but a few days! I had prepared myself to create a masterpiece, and now I could watch it reach fruition. Kolacka, yes. My diamond-in-the-rough, to be cut to my oh-so-delicate specifications, an indispensable linebacker with enough guile to deceive the devil himself. I could picture him laughing at my proposition. And the stolid, square Chuck Noren, a rock in the center of the offensive pit. No position could be better—or less conspicuous—than his, with innumerable ways to destroy an offensive drive, everything from a faulty block to an ever so slight breach of timing to, perhaps most damaging of all, a poorly centered snap on a field goal or an extra point.

Kolacka and Noren. I had seldom seen them together except in a large group, and never as intimates. They were such different types, I doubted that they'd ever spoken together as person to person, or shared opinions on anything. An absolutely perfect duo for my purposes.

Indeed, it was the mark of my progress that I'd come this far in a very short week. I felt much like Agatha Christie's Inspector Poirot as he closed in on his murder suspects with a grand design that built to a logical inevitability. The process was fascinating, and a mark of my confidence that I could enjoy the drama of it. Actually, I had often considered the possibility of initiating a book project as a member of a detective squad, presumably to see how adept I might be in solving a crime. The amateur sleuth in the world of New York's finest. I had actually fantasized that, given the opportunity and proper support, I could do a creditable job. Why not? I mused. Why not?

I was a forty-year-old tiger and there was nothing I could not do.

Even the sound of the ringing telephone was welcome now, and I reached for it with the sharpness of a man for whom living was a glorious adventure.

"Hello, there," came the sing-song voice that was the greatest treat of all. Patricia. After all, who else did I want to have calling?

I was in her room at the Beverly Hills Hotel as quickly as the freeways permitted.

Finally, there she was, smiling like a Cheshire cat as if all the mysteries of her appearance—and remoteness—were none of my affair. I did not comment, preferring to play this scene with the confidence of a born winner. I would go whichever way she wished.

She wanted to know all about "our little adventure" as she called it. She sat across from me in the living room of her suite, legs crossed, a cigarette in a long jeweled holder, eagerly waiting for details. So I gave her a full recounting, omitting nothing, just as any businessman might do for his partner. If I had to win her with the words of my scheming, so be it. The amorous finale would be the reward. Indeed, I was eloquently informative and appropriately amusing. She listened with the enthusiasm of a giddy little schoolgirl, constantly laughing at all the right places. It would seem that the fix was actually a lark. For all the dramatics of my week, nothing came out with any seriousness, and I could not help but wonder if this was not, indeed, its essence.

"Absolutely fascinating!" she exclaimed.

"You never doubted it, did you?"

"Well, it did seem rather nebulous. . . ."

She wanted to know more about Kolacka and Noren, especially Kolacka. She even probed for information on precisely how he would play—and what she might watch for. The very thought of the coming game became all the more exciting to her.

Then there came a time when I could wait no longer. I simply crossed the six or eight feet between us and firmly pulled her up from the chair. She did not resist. In fact, she looked up at me with a lovely inviting smile, and I sensed how dreadfully I'd missed her.

I felt strange, on the brink of some new plateau of emotion. She lifted her face to mine, sharing my anticipation in a prelude to our passion. Our kiss was so enriching, I could barely cope with it. I just wanted to hold her to me, and we clung to each other, fingers pressing into clothing as though digging for flesh.

I spoke her name and it sounded like a sigh. She responded, moving her lips back to mine, and this time the kiss was more demanding. I led her into the bedroom where slowly, with exquisite sensuality, she stepped out of her skirt.

"Take me, Gordon," she whispered.

I must say, it was awesome. I was alive to its impact at the very first contact of our bodies. The power of all my anticipations was omnipresent, that fantastic sense of fulfillment which transcends even one's wildest hopes. It was if nothing better would ever happen to me than what I felt at this moment with her. We feasted on the feel of each other, so full of a mutual hunger, it seemed insatiable. Each touch was electric, each kiss a probing for something more. Her soft sweet moans were as caresses. I'd never heard such sounds before. I whispered her name again and again as if the saying of it lent a special beauty to each new kiss it inspired. And when she spoke mine, it sent fresh tremors through me, stirring my erection to an intensity beyond anything I'd ever known.

When finally we copulated, she cried out through the lengthy ride, tears running down her lovely face as we flung our bodies at each other. There was no part of her that was not throbbing with passion. I drank her tears and sighed at the taste of her, driving into her with so much joy, I could not bear the thought that this would ever end. Indeed, I resisted the irresistible with all my strength, tightening buttocks, gnashing teeth, constricting loins until her own ecstatic screams sent shock waves through me and I exploded inside her mumbling words of love.

After, my head was reeling in a carousel room. I shut my eyes and buried my face in her neck, needing to hear her continuing sighs. We held each other, saying nothing that might break this spell. And then time forced a confrontation with reality.

"Oh, my . . ." she said, like one awakening to discover how late it was, and I found myself caught by a spasm of depression. The very thought of Lester with this woman became so distasteful, I did not believe I could possibly adjust.

Abruptly, she left the bed for the bathroom without a word, jarring me with her sudden indifference. In one quick second, the entire scene had changed its coloration. I lay there with my gathering doubts, wondering at the scope of my feelings, confused at the depth of them. When she emerged and re-dressed, I wanted to say things to her but, by the look of her, thought better of it.

Pat had no such problems. She seemed totally delighted at the whole affair.

"It's really been wonderfully exciting, Gordon. I can't tell you how much I look forward to the game."

"Well, yes, it will be fun. . . ."

Business before pleasure, then after, again. Business was not just business, business was also her pleasure. It really galled me. I had a horrid notion that her new interest in football might actually bring her closer to Lester. I didn't want to think about it, and jumped out of bed.

"I'll call you tomorrow," she said.

"Fine."

"And good luck!" she added with a bright, charming smile.

18

Back at the Glendale Arms, I went straight to the bar, where a number of Bulls could be found behind countless bottles of beer, struggling through another evening of their discontent. From the sublime to the ridiculous, I thought.

There were always a few strangers hanging around, out-of-town football fans attracted by the prospect of some small intimacy with the greats to take home with them. One such garrulous Southerner was constantly around, overeagerly soliciting their attention with that false bravado that pretends at being equal.

"Boy, you guys really have the life."

"No question," Chuck Noren said in exaggerated agreement. "We footballers are the happiest creatures on God's green earth."

"The way I heard it," the fan went on, "you play no more than seven or eight minutes of football a game, and you'll make $15,000 each if you win. Do you realize that comes to almost $2,000 a minute!"

"Is that so? I never thought of it that way," said Chuck. "Did *you*, Tiny?"

LaTourette shook his head. "All I can think about is the Thursday rule."

"What's that?" the fan was suckered into asking.

Tiny sighed with the despair of one to whom the very mention of this was a traumatic experience. "Starting tonight, Thursday, no man on this club is permitted to have intercourse until after the game."

"No shit!" the fan exclaimed.

"You see, Mr. Stillson has a theory about aggression, that the enjoyment of sex depletes it. And he's right, you know?" He turned to Kling, Baletti, Noren, and the others, and, of course, they all agreed. "Mr. Stillson explained that when you're sexually frustrated, you become violent; the more frustrated, the more violent. By Sunday, we're all like real killers. Raving mad killers. And that's because not a single man-jack on the squad had gotten laid for the previous three nights!"

"Well! . . ." the fan was beaming.

"Mr. Stillson told us how he was in the army, and the Japs were the greatest fighters in the war. They were unbelievable, the way they'd throw themselves into mine fields, machine gun fire, anything, the toughest little bastards you'd ever want to see. You want to know why? Because the night before the attack they were shown cock movies. After all those weeks of sexual denial, why, it transformed them into savages."

"Say, I'd heard something about that. . . ."

"I'll tell you a secret," Chuck interceded. "But you gotta promise not to repeat it. Okay?"

"Well, certainly."

"In the locker room, just before game time, we don't have those prayers you hear about. Don't you believe that stuff about us football players getting down on our knees;

that's all bullshit, mister. What Mr. Stillson does is turn out the lights and show us cock and cunt! For three solid minutes, we see movies of big pricks ramming into succulent snatches . . . all angles, mister, black pricks, white pricks, beautiful golden asses . . . I mean, *it really fires you up!*"

"Holy smoke!"

"But for three days, it's not easy. . . ."

"No, it ain't," Tiny picked it up. "I mean, I got this problem with my wife. Like she wakes up sometimes around one or two A.M., and she forgets it's Friday or Saturday, and she starts playing around. Well, maybe I get confused too, I mean, my cock don't know nothing about the calendar, and I get a big bone up, right? Now, what am I supposed to do? I mean, Jesus, a man can lose a lot of sleep with a big bone up."

Chuck simulated a deep moment of thought, twirling his beer bottle on the plastic table top. "Looks like you better sleep separate, Tiny."

"But there's only one bed."

"Get your wife to sleep on the floor."

"Aw, Chuck, I can't do that to her."

"Then *you* sleep on the floor."

"I tried that, but what happens is, I get that big bone up just thinking about *why* I'm there."

"What do you do then, get back in the hay with her?"

"Heck, no, 'cause I'd end up violating the rule. I stay right there and start whacking the big bone against the rug. Sometimes I have to whack it for an hour or so. Once I whacked it so hard, I woke up Doc Knowland in the room below. And my wife, she hears me, she gets out of bed to help me, you know, she whacks it for me because she can't sleep with all that racket neither. Well, finally, maybe it's two, three in the morning, I cream all over the damn rug, I'm all sweated up like I just ran a couple of miles. So I take a shower, right? But that wakes me up real good and I can't go back to sleep until maybe five A.M. So when I show up at breakfast looking like I'd been pumping 90 proof sourmash and chasin' ass all over the state, what do you think happens? Stillson sees me and says, 'LaTourette, you look beat, and I know why: you had multiple sex with your wife last night in violation of the Thursday rule, for which I'm fining you $500!' "

"Wow, you sure got a problem. . . ."

"God *damn.* It's rough. . . ."

Here, Gino Baletti had a suggestion. "Why don't you get your wife to fix herself up to look terrible. You know, curlers in the hair, creamy junk on her face. Maybe you can feed her some beans or something so she farts in bed. I mean, I, for one, can't stand a woman who farts in bed. There are ways, Tiny. Lots of ways. You wouldn't *want* to fuck her. You couldn't *possibly* get a hard-on."

"Man, it's dark in bed. I mean, she ain't no beauty to start with."

"Leave the lights on, then."

"Sleep with the lights *on?*" Tiny seemed appalled at such a thought.

"Why not? You'll take one look and your cock will disappear."

"Maybe I'll try that. . . ." Then, an afterthought: "What else besides beans? She don't like beans."

"Oatmeal cookies ain't bad."

"Why don't you ask Doc Knowland for a fart pill?"

"What?"

"They're terrific. They create real noisy farts. Ask Kling. He used to give 'em to his wife regular."

"That's right," Kling agreed. "That was before."

"Before what?"

"Before I learned how to use ice."

"Ice?"

"Yeah, ice. I get this large plastic bag, fill it with crushed ice, then secure it around my cock and balls like a huge jock. Just before bedtime. Works perfectly. Absolutely impossible to get a hard-on."

"Jesus!" cried out Tiny.

"See?" Chuck said. "You don't have to make a big thing of it."

The fan had taken it all in, too intrigued to suspect the put-on. He had turned full cycle from envy to outright pity.

"You poor bastards . . ."

"Yeah," Chuck sighed, "sometimes I think I can't stand it anymore."

There was silence for a moment, then Tiny glanced at his watch.

"Hey, it's almost eleven!"

They all jumped, knocking over chairs as they scrambled to their feet, raced upstairs to their rooms.

Reality fusing with fantasy, I mused. Bedcheck was usually a farce anyway, unless Lester himself conducted it. There were simply too many ways to fool the more casual coaches—everything from stuffing the bedclothes to simulate sleeping bodies to hiring hotel employees (sometimes women) to go to bed for them (at $5 an hour) until that telltale flashlight swept the room. Coaches were reluctant to awaken the men. Stillson, however, knew all the tricks and made absolutely certain who was in each bed.

I lingered for a while, enjoying the silence, recapturing recent dialogue for my notes. When I finally returned to my room, I was thinking about Patricia.

It was shortly after midnight when Jake Kolacka walked in. He said nothing, just crossed to the window, parting the curtains for a look at the pool as if a midnight show were going on for his benefit.

Finally, he broke the silence.

"He found me out."

"What! How is that possible!" I struggled for innocence.
"He said *you* fingered me, Gordon."

I must have turned pale. It was a prospect that never occurred to me, and it made my stomach flutter audibly. I leaned back against the wall for support, bringing a finger to rub my eye in hopes of concealing the shock.

I rallied my equanimity and attacked.

"That man will stop at nothing," I said. "He called me in this afternoon. It was quite marvelous, the way you'd intimidated him. He was really quite out of his head. He wanted to know what I knew. Anything at all. I said I knew nothing, I didn't know what he was talking about. Since he knew we were friends, he pumped me. Kolacka this, Kolacka that. Once a crook, always a crook. That sort of thing. I told him I thought he was out of his head, that when he calmed down, he'd have a better perspective on things. Even Ed Mann agreed with that."

"Mann also said you fingered me."

"Well, that's what Stillson told him to say. My God, Jake, you didn't believe them, did you!"

He stood there staring at me, his huge hairy arms folded across his chest. I had the feeling that everything depended on his answer.

"Well, you know I didn't, old buddy. . . ."

There was such warmth in his voice, my relief was consummate. Once again, I had handled a crisis with admirable dispatch.

"Who could have tipped him?" I asked. "I mean, I've heard he has spies on the club."

He shrugged as though it were a matter of no great importance.

"Probably Noren. Once a rat, always a rat."

"What!"

"Noren is a snitch. My guess is he gets paid by the fucking word."

"But he *hates* Stillson. He told me so a dozen times!"

Kolacka grinned. "He tells you what you want to hear. Then he kisses Lester's hairy ass."

"Are you sure, Jake?"

"Inka dinka doo," he sang.

I struggled to contain my anxieties. The implications, to say the least, were frightening. No sooner had I lit a cigar to suggest indifference when he hit with the most telling blow of all.

"I'll tell you what was crazy, Gordon. Old Lester was laughing about the whole thing."

"Stillson was *laughing*?"

"Yeah. He had no real proof that I'd done it, he said, but listen to this, Gordon: *even if I had,* he wasn't going to do anything about it. He said he had to admit it was the damnedest stunt he'd ever seen. 'It was a gem!' he said. How do you like that, old buddy. He said it was a goddam gem!"

He was beaming now. It was as though this were the most rewarding part of the entire experience.

"He even shook my hand, Gordon. He said I should be proud of myself!"

I tried to smile at Kolacka and his victory, but I was taking a bad beating. Kolacka was shaking his head like one whose incredulity would never wear off.

"I was thinking, Gordon—I know it sounds wild—but maybe that guy ain't so bad after all. . . ."

I was crushed. It had always seemed startling to me that words could have so great a physical impact. Had Kolacka driven his fist into my stomach, I doubt if I would've been as breathless or experienced any greater pain. He had exposed a simple thought, a momentary notion, indeed, it was hardly even a categorical statement, yet I was all but completely wiped out by it. Even at that instant, I could foresee how devastating the impact would be.

Noren and Kolacka, both.

Lester Stillson had all but knocked me out of the box.

19

Friday (Two Days to Go)

I had a terrible dream that night. I was scaling a rocky peak, higher and higher, until I found myself clinging to a precipitous crag from which I could not move. I looked down and saw a thousand-foot drop and knew I was doomed. In all my life, I never experienced such fear. I suffered a complete disintegration of self-control, a confrontation with certain death that was so real, I could barely breathe. I tried to maneuver, shaking and sobbing like a baby until I simply gave up on myself, and I fell screaming toward the jagged rocks below.

I awoke in a terrible sweat, hardly able to believe I was alive. I had never experienced anything comparable. It was barely five A.M., and I sat nursing a drink of Scotch. I knew only too well what had brought this on. Had I not suffered through several nights of increasingly confusing bouts with my bed? I was, of course, paying my dues. I suppose I could admit it to myself: I was all washed up. The one-two punch of Noren and Kolacka was more than punishing, it was an omen, the handwriting on the wall. Too much, too much. I now doubted my capacity for all this Machiavellia. One does not take on tasks that run counter to the demands and limitations of one's psyche.

I found myself wallowing in self-denigration. Was all this remorse brought on by a case of troubled nerves or a case of troubled conscience? If I had not misplayed the Kolacka hand, would I have managed to dream less intimidatingly? Or was I kidding myself? Indeed, had I been kidding myself with this project right from the beginning, *pretending* I could pull it off?

Whatever, I now knew I had best be done with the entire scheme. There would be no fixing of the Superbowl. There would be no further attempts at master criminality.

Fix the Superbowl? It was, after all, an absurdity. I wondered how I could have let such idiocy ever invade my thoughts, that grotesque fantasy inspired by a day of infamy. Fix the Superbowl! I let the words roll over my brain. Even the word "fix" seemed distasteful. Had I not always deplored the very sound of it? With all its multiple meanings, it was hardly a word at all. *Fix* a tire. *Fix* a traffic ticket. *Fix* a dog. What a *fix* to be caught in. I need a *fix*. I'll *fix* your wagon.

When I rethought how close I came to propositioning the likes of Chuck Noren, there was nothing left of my sensibilities.

I was definitely finished with it.

Having made that life-saving determination, lo, there was magic relief in its acceptance. Sick as I was, I felt like a free man again.

I was not unaware of complications. The crestfallen look on the face of Patricia Stillson, for example. In light of all her enthusiasm, what could I say to her? And what, precisely, would it do to her feelings about me?

The prospect of *that* defeat was not easy to take. It was a tribute to my resourcefulness, then, that I could take pride in it: was I not sacrificing my romance for a greater truth? Would it not be the ultimate folly to pursue what was destined for tragic defeat in order to protect a selfish need?

Patricia, Patricia, I could not love you, dear, so much loved I not caution more. . . .

I felt renewed. My strength was such that nothing could challenge it. I had shed my corruptions and acknowledged my follies. Best of all, I saw no reason why I could not satisfy all those justifiable antipathies to Lester in my book. After all, the very premise of my profession was that the pen was mightier than any shiv. I would destroy him with words, then.

There was no way to feed into a computer the level of relief induced by that decision. For a man whose psyche had betrayed him in the night, I was an absolutely sprightly fellow at breakfast. I looked forward to the day with the luxurious feel of a vacationer on a lark. At morning practice, I got a laugh surreptitiously mimicking the apelike walk of Jud Kling himself, a tactic I never would have dared to attempt before. I even had Sy Getz confused when he saw me dancing the Hustle to background rhythms as I moved from one laundry bin to another. In fact, I had all I could do to maintain a semblance of my normally lugubrious look less the omniscient Lester Stillson suspect me of some fresh duplicity.

Friday was also a day for various pursuits outside the locker room. First of all, I visited Jo Jo Abels in the Los Angeles County Hospital, in part out of compassion, but mostly out of curiosity.

"You look like you lost a battle with a Sherman tank," I said.

He was pleased to see me, shook hands with his left, for his right arm was in a cast up to the elbow. His head was bandaged, his nose and right eye as puffy as a battered boxer's.

"I'll be all right," he said.

"What happened to the other guys?" I quipped.

"Man, they zapped me from behind! I never drink, just a few beers. I was dancing with my woman, that's all, dancing. I went to the can for a piss and two punks came at me with cop clubs."

"Why?"

"Ask Stillson, the motherfucker."

"What!"

"His goons, man."

"But why?" I was skeptical. "Hadn't he hurt you enough by firing you?"

"Not if a nigger wants to talk about it. And this is one nigger who had some real talking to do. Man, I was going on TV. I was gonna tell what that lying sumbitch does to a man. Not just to me, to *ever'one*!"

He had a few local TV and radio interviews scheduled, mostly on black-oriented programs, but the sleazy stigma of the "drunken brawl" had stripped him of credibility, he was told. Now, he was "just another street nigger" to them.

I believed him. The whole story made sense enough. Lester frees a trusted old hand then has him beaten up for protesting. It had a sensational quality, eminently exploitable, and I started fabricating dramatic pictures of Jo Jo, swathed in bandages and plaster casts, pointing his *j'accuse* in Lester's face before the cream of the football world.

I jumped at it.

"Jo Jo, how would you like two tickets to the big Superbowl party tonight? I can offer you a first-rate audience of the biggest reporters in the country. They'll listen, I promise. You'll be the talk of the party!"

He smiled. I laid the pair on the bed, knowing I'd have no trouble replacing them. I could really look forward to the evening now.

It was, in fact, a day of miniparties that built up to the gala, all related to the Superbowl and hence directly related to my book. Before my recent epiphany, I'd chosen to avoid the frills of that scene, primarily because they would distract me from the urgency of my scheming. Now, however, I looked forward to them for the very same reason.

No story about the Superbowl could logically omit the nature and scope of its sociology. An all-American phenomenon. Only when one arrives at the Century Plaza Hotel in what Angelinos call Century City does this become fully apparent. The huge hotel was like a convention center for the game and its glamorous appurtenances. The press was quartered here, almost a thousand sportswriters from all over the country luxuriously billetted through the auspices of the National Football League with access to hundreds of typewriters and special communications lines to their respective media, day-and-night bar with steam tables loaded with huge roasts and hors d'oeuvres and salads. So, too, was CBS, the Superbowl network of the year, with its complement of several hundred executives, staff, and crew. Another huge and active group represented NFL Properties, Inc., who had booked 350 rooms themselves, a multimillion-dollar operation that tied in promotions of such companies as Nestles, International House of Pancakes, du Pont, Union Carbide, Standard Brands. Celebrities were there, from such dignitaries as the United States Secretary of the Interior, an ex–college football player himself, who would speak the glories of the game at luncheon festivities, to top Hollywood stars, who willingly lent themselves to the daily entertainments.

Superbowl was for the corporate elite. The power people dominated the entire city this week, for such was the distribution of Sunday's tickets. Controlled by the NFL and its sponsors, 80 percent of the tickets were never made available to the average fan. The others could watch it on TV—accompanied by an onslaught of commercials.

Football stars from noncompeting teams circulated through the meetings and parties, many in the temporary employ of a major company ($1000 for their services over the weekend, all expenses paid), for which they would chat with the company's guests as experts, escorting them to parties and to meet other sports celebrities, taking them golfing, drinking, whoring. There were also a few Superbowl players around, either to make their own business contacts or sell a portion of the twenty-five tickets given them. (Priced at $25 each, the good ones were marketable at $150 a pair—though scalping was in direct defiance of NFL ethics.)

But it was the parties that excited them all, lavish bacchanalia that appeared to transcend time and locale, social-sexual-business spectaculars designed to make the weekend indelibly memorable, beginning with an amiable discussion with Walter Cronkite, say, then working all the way up to a superexotic experience befitting the super occasion. "An orgy of excess" was the most-used phrase. It was estimated that upwards of $25,000,000 would be spent in Los Angeles this week, most of it flowing from the bottomless purses of corporate tax-deductible expense accounts. This was where the real ball game was being played, these gentlemen (and their ladies), the Superbowl sponsors who would pay as much as $230,000 for the showing of a one-minute commercial. And here were the gentlemen from CBS, who, having presented the NFL with a $4,000,000 check for the rights to broadcast the game, then sold over thirty minutes for commercials—totaling almost $8,000,000 in TV time, all based on the assumption that a substantial number of the 90,000,000 viewers would go out and buy what they'd been instructed to buy.

The network was proud of its own expenditures, issuing

press releases that its TV staff on Sunday would number well over 200, that there would be 18 cameras, 100 monitors, and over 7 miles of cable—so much equipment that they'd rented enough trailers to populate a small village.

All this, then, was grist for my writing mill, and I spent the bulk of the day at a round of parties, escalating, at last, to the NFL Superspecial $250,000 affair on the old MGM lot.

It was beyond opulence. Several thousand people were invited to a vast sound stage now decorated in the tradition of one of those great Hollywood musicals. Chandeliers hung from the towering roof, simulated marble pillars held up glittering balconies, wide staircases spiraled down from magnificently draped stages beside cascading fountains. There were four bands alternating different musical styles from Dixieland to country rock. Huge tables offered succulent roasts and casseroles, and champagne flowed from every vantage point.

The bands played, vocalists sang. Beautiful people in brightly colored finery mingled in the classic postures of a cocktail party, chatting while an eager eye roved to see whom they might chat with next. My own eyes kept scanning the multitude for a large black man swathed in bandages. To abet this search, I'd tipped a few hired hands to be on the lookout, advising them where I might be found.

"How are you, Eddie?" I asked an old sportswriter I hadn't seen in months.

"I hear this is Pete Rozelle's third party of the evening," he said, raising his glass.

"How does it look to you Sunday?"

"One write-in vote for the old Green Bay Packers."

It was like that. The party had nothing to do with the coming game.

Well, I would change that. At least insofar as Lester Stillson was concerned. The notion of a man like Jo Jo making a big scene at such a party was the dynamic stuff of dreams. A clash of opposites, as it were. The battered and abused ballplayer taking the hated tormenter to task. One could easily predict the response of the sportswriters, suddenly routed from the boredom by Lester's hooliganism.

"I'll see you later, Eddie."

I saw Joe Weed. He was as surly as ever.

"I wonder what the poor people are doing tonight," he said.

"Waiting for your column tomorrow."

"Look at them. The football fans. Huhn, they know football the way I know the theory of relativity."

I floated in a maze of minidialogues.

"I hear this is Pete Rozelle's fifth party of the night."

There were always a few running backs with a kind word for Jud Kling. "He's mean, all right. He's so mean he kicks the shit outta *himself.*"

"Man, he comes at you so fast, you don't have time to close your eyes!"

"I understand Kling was once a 97-pound weakling."

"Yeah, when he was three."

In the presence of women, the talk was mostly about football with overtones of fear. Alone, football players talked mostly about women.

"Some reporter asked me did I ever have nightmares before a game. I told him, hell, no, you gotta be able to *sleep* first."

"I got this steel pin in my shoulder now. It hurts a little, but I get great reception on my car radio."

The irritant becomes a joke in the jargon of the oppressed.

Then there were those who talked exclusively about money.

"Last year I made almost a hundred grand. I spent 90

percent of it on clothes, fast cars, dames. The other 10 percent I just pissed away."

"I heard once that when Babe Ruth made eighty grand, it would be worth three hundred grand today, figuring taxes and inflation. I figured, if *I* was playing then, I'd've been making about eleven cents a day."

"I'll tell you something: I've given football ten of the best years of my life. Now I'm gonna give a few of my lousy ones."

The 2500 guests circulated like browsers at a flea market, gaping at this one and that one in an endless hunt for celebrities. Since it was a party of limited invitations (tickets were as difficult to come by as game seats at the Coliseum), we were all endowed with a sense of importance.

But where was Jo Jo Abels?

The gentlemen of the press were all too quickly drunk. They had been circulating through this sprawling city for over a week, fully aware of their uselessness until Sunday. (Said one: "I've learned how to swallow my pride: just chew on it first.") What one felt here was an overpowering futility.

I joined a group of them. They had settled at tables with their wives and uncommonly tall highballs. It was a mark of their fatigue that they preferred to reminisce rather than speculate on the immediate future, less concerned with Cowboys or Bulls than last year's gala party or the relative desirability of New Orleans over Houston as a Superbowl city.

"No contest: New Orleans by ten points," said one.

"Dunno 'bout that. Houston is the most underrated overrated city in Texas."

"If I may paraphrase the great Sonny Liston, I'd rather be a lamppost in New Orleans than mayor of Houston."

That settled, they went on to more vital issues. For example: "I said to Mickey Mantle, 'What are you doing these days?' He tells me, 'I'm VP in marketing. That means I play golf and go to cocktail parties.' I said, 'I'll bet you're damned good at your job.'"

"I called my wife last night, and she told me her American Express card was stolen. You know something? The goddam thief will probably spend less than she does."

"Hey, there's Pete Rozelle. Somebody said that this was his *ninth* party of the evening!"

"Who in hell is Pete Rozelle?"

They laughed.

I excused myself, feigning a need to return to the festive board, but actually to seek out Jo Jo Abels. Again, to no avail.

"Dammit, I'm going into training tomorrow," someone was saying. "I'm gonna quit the booze and do some jogging."

"What in hell for?"

"I've got to work myself up for the game."

Somebody immediately poured him a fresh drink.

Joe Weed, by then, was almost totally smashed, achieving a sublime state of lucidity.

"The world is full of shits, pricks and cocksuckers," he began.

"They all sound the same to me," commented somebody's wife.

"No, ma'am, there are important distinctions: the shit will make your life miserable, then feel sorry for you. The prick will fuck you up, and couldn't care less. But the cocksucker, he *deliberately* sets out to destroy you and *loves* every minute of it."

"Lester Stillson," everyone acknowledged.

It was like magic. Even before the laughter had subsided, he was standing beside us, arms akimbo, no doubt the only man in this giant hall without a drink in his hand.

He was clearly there to confront me. "I'm told you've

been looking for poor Jo Jo Abels. Well, he couldn't make it, Gordon. The doctor insisted he stay in bed."

The report was such a sudden intrusion on my expectations, I needed a moment to handle it. And into the vacuum came Stillson himself.

"You're really not very smart, Littlefield. Typical of bleeding hearts like you. You punks hate dirty tricks except when you can play them."

I seethed, but held my temper. I told myself that it was a small thing. I need not be concerned. It really did not matter at all. I even went beyond such palliatives, reminding myself of the follies that had resulted from earlier rages. Let him have his petty victories. Surely, no one present would judge me poorly for my silence.

Then I thought of Patricia and was washed by a wave of jealousy. There was no way I could contain the anger that crept up on me, irritating the nerve endings. All I could think of was that he had beaten me again.

He was laughing as he turned to leave, that quick abrasive cackle of his, and I lost my stomach for silence.

"Lester, goddammit, what did you do to him!" I snapped with such venom, I could feel the others staring at me in amazement.

When he faced me again, he wore the look of one who could see right through me. A crusher, as it turned out, for I could see right through myself. I was using Jo Jo. I was playing with pipe dreams of Patricia. The outburst was a distortion, a warping of intelligence. I was becoming a puppet to my rage.

He laughed again. It was as though he had planned the entire maneuver.

"What did *I* do to him? I didn't even see him. *You* did."

"Did you have him beat up again? Or drugged maybe?"

"Oh, come off it, Littlefield. Why don't you stick to writing. Put it all in your book, if you're so hot about it. I suggest you also put in that it was Lester Stillson who kept old Jo Jo in pro football his last three years when no one else would have a nigger accused of raping a white school teacher!"

I was stopped. I looked around for support. Joe Weed, red-eyed and flaccid, was nodding. "He tells it like it is," he said.

Lester grinned, and I braced myself.

"What you don't understand, Littlefield, is that I think of everything. *Everything.* That's why I win. That's why I'm gonna win on Sunday. And when I do, that makes everything else right. And that's what punks like you will never understand!"

This time he left, and I was buried in silence. There seemed to be something terribly significant happening here, something to do with my pride and credibility. Less than two weeks ago, I'd walked off that squash court and played a comparable scene. A memory of that cold shower came back to me with all those glorious aspirations. I was losing too many battles, wasn't I? Could I stand under an icy spray tonight? Even if I got smashed?

This awareness of my fragility was sickening. In my brooding self-pity, I kept returning to thoughts of Patricia, of fondling those warm and responsive breasts as I breathed in the exquisite fragrance of her silken hair. I was ready to settle for that, wasn't I, as though all other goals could be abandoned for the satisfactions of once having had her. I had been beaten, not as much by Lester as by myself, compounding my subjugation by wallowing in it like a romantic fool. It was pathetic.

I lifted myself from this setting of humiliation to seek solace in anonymity, ending up in a sleazy bar on Pico Boulevard, its color TV flashing screeching tires and gunplay, a sordid setting that complemented my mood. I took two double Scotches to an empty booth, sat with my back to the TV, and pretended I could drink my troubles into oblivion.

But the alcohol failed to dampen the fires, it ignited them. My frustrations took on a new meaning, provoked a whole new mood. Instead of sinking into a quagmire of self-pity, I rose to a new combativeness. Instead of a sustained hopelessness, there was a regeneration of rage. Sure, I took warning that this was false and illusory, the kind of courage that came out of the bottle and all that nonsense. Many a drunk suddenly thought he was Superman and jumped off the roof believing he could fly. I didn't care about that. What mattered was that I didn't want to quit. Not under Lester's snickering arrogance. I was going to take him, even though he had me over a barrel with a gun aimed at my anus. I would attack, just as I'd planned. I would rely on my talents to whip him, no matter what cards he held.

And I would too, by God. Exactly the way I'd planned it.

That was it, all right. I actually laughed into my Scotch, splattering my face with cool bubbles. As I wiped them off, I knew I would always remember that, too.

For this was the second time I'd decided to fix this game.

20

"A foolish consistency is the hobgoblin of little minds" wrote Ralph Waldo Emerson. I would bathe in that quote as I rallied my forces again. If I had lost precious time in the day of my divertissement, I had certainly regained an equally precious determination.

Two names. I needed two names. For all the complexity, I was up for it. The momentum had changed again, and I was riding the crest of my eagerness to win.

So I burst into my room much like a poet driven by some rarely achieved inspiration and warmed up my pen with a few relevant doodles:

> A name, a name, what's in a name?
>
> The name of the game
> Is the name *for* the game.
>
> The proper nomen
> Is a happy omen.
>
> Foolish nominations
> Make
> Ghoulish abominations.

Hold a candle
To his handle.

The majesty and daring of a matador's veronica
Is trivia in contrast to the perfect proper monicker.

I laughed, tucking away this page of couplets as a memento for my anticipated triumphs. Then, remembering an old Philo Vance mystery wherein that master detective used just such a doodle to solve a crime, I tore the page into a tiny pile of scraps and set fire to it.

Again, I laughed, all charged up for what I had to do. Time had run out on me—or was about to—stripping me of the luxury of any further procrastination. The moment of truth had arrived and, by God, I was thoroughly prepared for it. I was the dedicated scholar walking into his final exam. I was the track star, finely tuned and all warmed up, approaching the starting line at the Olympics. I was the great violinist about to walk on stage for a long-awaited recital.

I was Gordon Littlefield III and I was going to do the impossible.

It was all quite marvelous for it came from the very core of me. Instead of panic, there was promise. There would be no cop-out tossing of coins when I made these selections, there would be no so-what, easy-come, easy-go sort of fatalism, no preconceived alibis to cover my pride in the event of disaster. The way I felt, I knew that my insights would be sharper than ever, that I was about to make the wisest and most perceptive decisions humanly possible.

So I confronted my charts for what promised to be the last time.

Starting with the offense, I stared at two encircled names: Perry Lee Stover, RG, and Willie Jones, TE.

Tight end, of course, was a position that offered far more destructive opportunities than any interior lineman. The quick short pop over the middle for five or six yards had to be Willie's forte, sometimes opening a series of downs, sometimes sustaining a drive with a desperately needed third down—and always a threat that kept linebackers sufficiently on edge to prevent them from destroying the running game. I could picture Willie making three or four such catches on Sunday, then allowing himself to get trapped in the coverage just long enough to miss a crucial pass—or allowing another to slip through his hands as he gets hit. I could also picture him missing a block as Ace Carter starts a third-down sweep. Willie's blocking was at least as important to the offense as his pass catching—especially when closing in on that goal line.

A guard, on the other hand, was not nearly as potentially dangerous to an offense's power. Certainly, not in so obvious a way. A guard opened the holes for power plays. He pulled to block out defensive ends and linebackers on sweeps. He fought giant defensive tackles nose to nose to keep them from smothering the quarterback on pass plays.

In this light, I leaned toward the tight end. Unlike a wide receiver, there was something very comforting about his confined existence. Though he was a ball handler, his work was generally performed in a crowd, and a most vicious crowd at that. No one would suspect a tight end of deliberately throwing a game because he failed to hang on to a pass with a 260-pound linebacker leaping on him.

Nonetheless, I was not entirely at ease with this. If this position was the better of the two, the choice of Willie over Perry Lee was less so. If Willie Jones' eruptive volcano had drawn me to him in the first place, it now gave me pause. Had he attacked Chuck Noren the other afternoon because he knew Noren was Stillson's spy? I pondered his dour inscrutable ways and did not trust those earlier instincts that made him seem so promising to me.

Had I tailored them to my needs in the enthusiasm of discovery? I now found myself picturing Willie plucking a pass off his shoe tops with one of his huge grasping hands, then stampeding through a gang of tacklers to go all the way in for six. Or, conversely, I saw him playing the fool, dropping a pass laid perfectly in his gut when such a play was totally unnecessary.

Perry Lee, on the other hand, seemed to be the perfect man for this season. For all his Bible-reading piety, I could smell his corruptibility. He would give me a workmanlike job, blessed with a solid motivation that was measurable in dollar bills. Not only did he hate Stillson, he hated his teammates for their unholy derisiveness. He would, in effect, put God on my side. Perhaps best of all, no one could possibly suspect a "deacon," especially one whose deceits were hidden in pile-ups. What it got down to, then, was my opting for the man rather than the position.

Yes, I would go with Perry Lee. And having made my decision, I began buttressing it with instant images of offensive breakdowns no one could possibly understand.

I lit up a Havana and relaxed in a cloud of soft white smoke. A time-out before taking on the defense.

What fascinated me now was another view of Jake Kolacka wherein I felt a lingering distrust of him. It was as though my decision to exclude him was actually an accumulation of dubious reactions. For all his marvelous deviltry, an unpredictable quality hung over him, that schizophrenic miasma, no doubt. It seemed to me, in a game as emotional and volatile as the Superbowl, Jake would become volatile and capricious. Without a proper hunger for money, he could conceivably become a man of art rather than of commerce. He would forget the money, forget Stillson, forget everything but his momentary responses on the field. I wanted a pirate, not a prankster. Or, to put my appraisal in popular vernacular, Kolacka was overqualified.

If not Kolacka, then who?

I had three names left on defense: Oscar Ayers, S, Tiny LaTourette, LE, and Ernie Snyder, CB. I stared at them as though the answer would leap out at me, lighting up in some mysterious glow. It didn't, of course, but it did not take long to eliminate two. LaTourette was nothing but a huge beast. I could not see myself approaching him. Not that he wasn't corruptible, but merely that I could not relate to him. At best, he would be a troublesome last resort.

Shifting to his blond, sadistic roomie, Ernie Snyder, I found even less satisfaction. He was a brilliant cornerback with the instincts of a great athlete, but I was put off by his flakiness. Another case where my demand for honor among conspirators drove me away from a man. I would say a strong preliminary no to Snyder, but was prepared to reappraise my opinion if necessary.

Which left me with Oscar Ayers, that catlike black with a grieving heart. I realized, at last, that I liked him. I liked his sophisticated cynicism. I even liked his admiration for the militant Henry Coll, and his friendship with Jo Jo Abels. I found a tremendous plus in his history as a great college quarterback and the denial of his rightful place when he made it to the pros. I relished his financial and emotional crisis inspired by his oncoming divorce and the alimony payments that would hang over him. I even liked the way he played football: daring, imaginative, instinctive. There was nothing ordinary about Oscar, least of all the pixielike intelligence of his pass coverage combined with the ferocity of his tackling. I especially liked his story of how he had once made four jolting tackles in a row, unprecedented for a safety, then limped off the field with two cracked ribs—only to be called "yellow" by Coach Seager and ordered back into the game—whereupon he simply walked straight into the locker room and quit for the day. I could feel confident with such a man.

It would be Oscar, then. Yes, I felt fine about Oscar.

Perry Lee and Oscar. The Deacon and the Cat. I poured myself an inch or so of Scotch and toasted my two colleagues in absentia. Immediately aglow, I poured another shot and toasted myself for the extraordinary acumen with which I had arrived at this. Exhausted now, I closed my eyes, not to sleep, but to play out a scenario in which the game action was mine to manipulate like a brilliant puppeteer. I had always been adept at creating fantasies, enjoying all manner of sensual and artistic triumphs. To be sure, I dreamed up a superb game, a thrilling game for all the world to see, perfectly manipulated by my two puppets right down to the final minute. The game ended 21–20 in favor of Dallas. I didn't even need the three points.

Finally, then, twenty-four hours after I'd fouled my bed, I returned to it, and I thought how wonderful it was that all things could change so remarkably in so short a time.

21

Saturday (One Day to Go)

It was never out of mind that I still had the enormously delicate problem of confronting these two men. Not only was there danger of rejection, but an accompanying threat of violence. A man like Perry Lee Stover could conceivably react with inhuman ferocity, so appalled at this devil's proposal that he would actually tear off my head. My estimation, of course, was quite the opposite, but how could I be sure of it?

With no small trepidation, then, I went to the attaché case for my cache of cash and its ready-to-bribe envelopes. I put one in my jacket and returned the case to the closet.

I was ready at last.

As I worked my chores at Saturday's practice, I learned first hand what "pregame anxiety" was like. Let it be known that this was no simple, ordinary workout, though it posed as such. There were forty-three men out there who had gone through a turbulent and chaotic season, a disparate group of dissidents who were barely capable of surviving even rudimentary sociability. On this day, strange things happened on that field. If, as usual, they snapped at each other as they ran through signals, their timing was excellent. On pass routes, nearly every pass hit target, and nothing was dropped, yet not a word was said to indicate their perfection. Coach Seager kept his mouth shut like one terrified of breathing lest it rock a leaky boat. And when they finished, they moved into the locker room as though they had just come away from some ignominious defeat. Even Jud Kling felt a need to mumble obscenities as if it actually hurt him to rip the tape from his ankles.

I maneuvered among them, picking up their sweat clothes in tactful silence, gradually weaving my way toward Perry Lee. I would begin here, with what I considered to be the tougher of my two choices, the way an offense will drive at the strongest member of the defense to establish its superiority. If I walked away with Perry Lee in the bag, the conquest of Oscar would seem trivial.

As usual, he handed me his money pouch to hold as he showered, not trusting the metal strongbox that Sy kept locked away. This time, I opened it, counting his meager sixteen dollars. Knowing he would check it out, I inserted an extra five dollars of my own on the belief that even so petty a discrepancy was apt to put him in a favorable frame of mind.

Minutes later, he came to collect it, a clean towel draped around his waist, his hairless muscular body smelling heavily of talcum.

"Only one more time," he said, taking back his pouch.

"You have made a deep impression on my pocket," I said.

He managed a smile, then furtively opened the pouch for a quick look-see. There was no question but that he saw the extra five, for Perry Lee was a man who handled money the way John Scarne handled a deck of cards. What amused me was the deftness with which he concealed his surprise, a quick cough, turning his head as though to shield me from it. I then offered him a ride back to the hotel, adding that there was something I wanted to talk to him about, achieving just the right level of mystery to entice him.

As I drove, I would have been more at ease with a good cigar in my mouth but I deferred to his abhorrence of such godlessness.

"I must say, Perry Lee, I've learned a lot from you...."

He seemed surprised at that—or, perhaps, skeptical of my intent. "How do you mean?"

"Frugality. I've decided I must learn to be more cautious about the way I spend my money."

"Ah'm grateful for your saying that, Gordon."

"Well, I admire the way you are."

Relieved, he contributed his own summation. "Ah'm not gonna be poor again. No suh!"

I had a vision of a stark, drab home within walking distance of everything, a wife in a wash-print dress, a handful of moppets trained to do chores.

"I hope you've had a chance to put something away after all these years," I said, knowing he'd been in the pros for eight, but I didn't want to suggest any expertise.

He shrugged, unwilling to discuss what had to be his best-kept secret. I could even presume that he would go home with his Superbowl check, take a day off to reorganize his family, then immediately go back to the work in the hardware store he owned. (Would he check the accounts before or after he made love to his wife?)

"An English writer named Somerset Maugham once wrote that 'money is like a sixth sense without which you cannot make use of the other five,'" I said.

He was fascinated by the quote, as I knew he would be.

"Would y'all say that again?"

I did, then watched him repeat the words to himself.

Twice, as a matter of fact. He savored it almost as though it were cash itself.

"It always intrigues me, what people do with their money," I went on.

"The wrong people have money," he offered. "Ah've seen it happen over 'n' over. Folks' heads git turned by it. They git to spendin' and sinnin' and then there's nothing left of 'em."

"Then there's Lester Stillson," I said. "He seems to feel that no one should have money except himself."

He grunted in agreement and we fell silent again. I let him play with his thoughts for a moment, then reopened the matter. "From what I gather, hardly a player among you hasn't suffered financially because of him."

Another grunt. This time, he made his own contribution. "My first year, ah hurt my knee real bad. I couldn't play. Everybody knew that. But Doc Knowland says to Stillson that ah *can* play, that way Stillson can cut me from the squad without paying me."

"And then he got you for less money the next year?"

"He always got me for less money. And he always had a new way to do it. Ah'd be asking a few thousand over the minimum and he'd holler at me like ah was actin' like some big shot quarterback!" He was hissing with rage now, eager to go on. "With Stillson, y'all play the interior line, you just a horse. He *tells* you that. How you gonna argue with a man like that?"

I nodded, and my throat was choking on the sixty-four-zillion-dollar question I was getting ready to pop. My natural proclivity was to take my time with such a matter. Perhaps throw a few more cliches around. Assure him of my kindred feelings. Titillate his hunger. Then I sensed its counterproductiveness, for, sooner or later, he was apt to suspect a ruse. So, tightening the muscles of my jaw, I swallowed the apple, as they say, and collected all my power to face this preposterous moment of truth.

"Perry Lee, I know a way to get back at that man."

"Sure would like to hear that."

"Do you have an idea how much he wants to win tomorrow's game?"

"Ah guess . . ."

"More than a young mother delivering her firstborn. More than a blind man yearning for sight."

I paused, struggling to achieve the right level of nonchalance. "You can take that away from him, Perry Lee. You can really break him, you know that? You can leave him simpering like a baby. You can do this and no one would know except you and I."

The words trailed off, barely audible, my voice dissolving in a flood of terror. I took a deep breath, finally letting out the words that could ignite black thunderclouds on majestic mountaintops. "Perry Lee, I can send you home with an extra fifty thousand dollars cash if you help me pull this off!"

With the courage of a great white hunter facing a charging hippo, I relaxed my foot on the accelerator and stared directly into Perry Lee's eyes. He was gasping for air. His beady blue eyes seemed to shrink in fear. The huge round pink face turned pasty white.

I fired another round. "Fifty thousand dollars, tax free. You'd be beating back the devil himself, Perry Lee. Fifteen thousand right now, thirty-five more tomorrow, after the game."

At last he spoke. Or tried to. His voice was hardly above a whisper, a feeble one at that. It was as though he were terrified that the car itself might be bugged.

"What the devil y'all talkin' 'bout?"

Immediately I knew I had him. His voice betrayed his approval. I turned away to conceal my satisfaction, concentrating on the road.

"We're gonna lose the game, Perry Lee."

"You mean *me*!"

"You and one other. On defense."

"Who?"

"You won't ever know his name. He won't ever know yours."

"But why me?"

"I trust you, Perry Lee. I believe you trust me in return."

"Well, yes . . ."

"It seems to me, you could easily stall an offensive drive without exposing yourself."

"I don't really know . . ."

"And no one would ever suspect you, would they?"

His wheels were spinning hard, as they say. I faced him again, this time with a reassuring smile. "I mean that as a compliment, you know."

He was still dumbfounded, much in the manner of one who'd just won a jackpot on a TV game show and didn't know quite how to react. I plowed into the breach as though it were all settled.

"The way I see it, the important thing is not to get a big jump on the Cowboys. I think it would be dangerous to score on our first drive, say. I realize there's just so much you yourself can do to stall it. You'd simply have to go with the feel of the game." Then, after another pause, "I mean, you could play a really fine game and look terribly good."

This time, a long silence. I thought of suggesting the most destructive tactic of all, nervously jumping into a penalty on third down and short yardage, but decided to wait. It was definitely his move now.

"S'pose it don't work? S'pose ah can't pull it off?"

"You get the fifteen thousand, and that's all. You'll notice that the big money comes only if you succeed. A proper inspiration, you might say."

He nodded. In fact, he kept nodding. Then he spoke the words that finally deflowered me: "Well, it *could* be done."

Immediately, I reached into my jacket pocket and withdrew the envelope. With the cool of one handing over a pack of cigarettes, I dropped it in his lap. I had intentionally left it unsealed that he might immediately see the substance within. One hundred and fifty $100 bills had to be a handsome sight to this man.

He saw it, all right. His hands appeared to tremble as he fingered through it. Then, satisfied, he took off his shoe and sock, pressed the envelope against the sole of his huge foot, then put them back on. As good as any bank, I suspected.

When he finished, I took my right hand off the wheel and extended it to him. We shook on it.

"Ah don't guess it'd be hard to do . . ." he speculated. "Like miss a block when Ace comes through my side. Maybe holding too much on pass blocking to draw a penalty . . ." Then, more positively as he got the feel of the venture: "On pitchouts and sweeps, I'm supposed to pull real quick. Ah mean, maybe Ah could be a mite late and jam up the blocking."

"That's the idea, Perry Lee."

His mind was moving with the potentials, so I let him alone. He would work it out without any further probing from me.

I wondered why I'd been so apprehensive about him.

Immediately, however, I began to worry about Oscar, a quantum leap from a hippo to a panther. Oscar Ayers, free safety, fast and powerful, surefooted and resourceful, constantly coming from nowhere to pounce on a helpless prey.

Oscar was a smartass, but a pliable one. His blackness

was a threat, but also a pose. His problem was that he had always lacked power. If I may reverse a famous aphorism, *lack* of power corrupts, and so on. My problem was to cut through the tortured communication of racial disparity and face him head on, pirate to pirate.

I saw him in the motel tavern with his cronies, a table full of beer bottles. I bided my time at the bar, nursing a Scotch, hoping for a convenient trip to the men's room that would find him there. Barely fifteen minutes went by before I was rewarded, and I slipped off the bar stool and casually followed him inside.

"What's happening, writer . . . ," came Oscar's routine greeting. We were side by side at the urinals.

"Feeble bladder, usually a sign of tension with me."

He laughed. "You feared of spillin' the Gatorade tomorrow?"

I maintained an earnest posture as though relieving myself were the sole matter of importance. "What I can't seem to cope with is all this emotion during the pregame period. You're going to be all juiced up, aren't you? . . . Oscar, I'd appreciate a few serious thoughts from you about this."

"Man, you gonna ask a nigger to *think*?"

Fortunately, he was eager enough to talk, inspired by an apparent show of nerves. As we went back to the tavern, he kept rambling on about how cool he was.

"But don't you really love the game? The excitement?"

"Man, I'm closing in on thirty. That hopped-up shit is for the kiddies. Ever'body trying to make out like the Superbowl is God's birthday. Sheeit, 'cept for the extra bread, it just another ballgame."

I didn't believe him for one instant, but I was pleased as punch that he chose to say it.

"You won't put out more?" I went on.

"I *hurt,* man. I got bruises on my bruises. Twenty-three

games since August. No, I don't love the fuckin' game. I don't love the fuckin' team. I don't know who the fuck I love. . . ."

Well, there it was again, the time to make my move. I slapped a few dollars on the table and slid off my chair.

"Oscar, let's talk upstairs."

"I like my beer, Gordon."

"I promise you something better."

In my room, I gave him a Havana cigar and a shot of Scotch. We sat back like bankers after a gourmet dinner.

"Yeah, it's better," he agreed, then laughed at the sight of himself in the mirror. "You full of shit, but you're something else, you know that?"

"I don't follow you, Oscar."

"What you got me up here for? You gonna write a story 'bout a pissed-off black dude?"

I was about to dive into a tank of sharks but it seemed almost like fun.

"Oscar, I'm curious: in all the years you've played football, were you ever approached to play less than your best?"

"You mean, dump?"

"Something like that."

He laughed. "Well, yeah. Once. To shave the points, you know?"

"But it wasn't your style?"

"Too much risk for too little money, I guess."

My cigar ash had grown to treacherous length, and I dangled it gently over the tray. "Suppose you were offered a *large* sum of money . . . just suppose."

He looked at me through the cloud of smoke, his eyes narrowing under deep furrows. The surly face worked slowly into a scowl, his mouth twisting from comedic to malevolent—or so I read it. Then suddenly the scowl turned into a grin and his eyes softened, and he began to laugh, just barely audible at first, then it grew, second by second, until he literally threw his head back and roared.

"Man, you sure something!" he said, laughing again. "You the fuckin'est cat I ever met!" Tears rolled down his face until they got lost in his wiry beard, for his hands were too occupied with drink and cigar to intercept them.

"Suppose you let me in on the joke," I said.

"*You*, man. *You're* the joke! The big fancy rich whitey literooman. You just another ratshit hustler looking for some action!"

It was my turn to scowl, but I was not about to begin a dialogue with him about this. "I was merely posing a question, Oscar."

"Well, tell me some numbers, okay? Then I'll pose you an answer."

I thought now how dangerous this man was—not that it mattered at this point. I told him the terms, the fifteen thousand first, the thirty-five more after the game, all the while careful to continue the charade of it being just a fantasy.

He absorbed them. "Fifty, eh . . ."

"That'd be more than you make all year," I suggested. "I mean, when you figure the tax problem . . ."

He was playing around with it, I could see that clearly enough. "It's like what you might call 'secret money,'" I added, referring to the alimony problems he was about to have. "It would all be in $100 bills, say. A man of your stature would have no difficulty handling them. A safe deposit box, that's all you'd need. No one would know. No one."

"Shut up a minute, will you?" He left the chair, taking the cigar and brandy with him for a walk to the window. I watched him, fully aware that I might be in trouble.

"How many you figure to get into this little 'make-believe' caper?" he asked.

"Just one other," and I explained the need for secrecy.

He thought about that, again taking his time. "I think it's nuts!"

"Perhaps. But don't tell me it couldn't work."

"Man, you got no idea the things that could happen out there!"

"Agreed. But the man with the money is taking the risks."

"Sure, sure. But he'll end up with money no matter what. The jock, he end up shoveling shit!"

I had to admit the truth of it. In fact, he had summed up the entire 1919 Black Sox Scandal in a dozen words.

"Oscar, any way you figure it, $35,000 extra for losing is a lot better than $7500 extra for winning . . . especially on this ballclub." Then I began to bait him with the challenge he'd have to face; I speculated on how he'd have to manipulate the pass coverage so that he'd not be suspect, a job that required even more mastery than playing straight. Or making a brilliant tackle, but just a hairline too late to stop a first down. "The way I see it, only a man of your experience could pull this thing off, Oscar. It may be the most difficult game you ever played!"

Still, he did not commit himself, and watching him, I began to feel the chilling premonitions of a loser. Suddenly desperate, I decided to take the big chance. I withdrew the sealed envelope from my pocket, slapped it on my open hand to draw his attention, then tossed it at him. He caught it easily enough but did not open it, weighing it for a moment. Suppose he takes it to Stillson and reports the entire conversation? Though it would be my word and reputation against his, he would have the envelope to back him. It was a gamble I had to take.

At long last, he put the envelope in his pocket, unable to contain a smile any longer. "You a very smart man, writer," he said.

"Let me freshen your drink," I said.

I accepted the victory with an easy grace, almost as

though I'd really expected it all along. Oscar was obviously pleased with the whole thing, a fresh unmistakable sparkle in his eyes, especially when I asked him how he thought he could handle the matter.

"Short-legging," he said.

Meaning, not running as fast as one could.

"A safety is the last to get a pop at the runner. He can miss a tackle and he goes in for six, or maybe catch him a little too late to stop a first down, that sort of thing."

"What about pass defense?" I asked.

"Sheeeit," he grinned. "I could fuck up coverage without the receiver even comin' into my zone."

"You won't have to fall down, or something so obvious?"

"Defensive backs fall down all the time, man. Get turned the wrong way, get tripped up. It happens."

"Well, make it look smart, Oscar."

"I'll play a helluva game."

He seemed pleased with himself now. So much so, it called for a caveat.

"You understand, you will do absolutely no betting. No tipping of friends, Oscar. The slightest word can come back to ruin you."

"No sweat," he said.

We toasted our collaboration and then fell silent. He sat down again, crossed his legs, sipped his drink with a pensive air.

"I was just thinking, man, how the world is one big shithouse."

And for me, an oyster, I thought.

With trumpets sounding glory in my ears, I went to call Patricia. Once again, I was the hero claiming his *droit du vainqueur*. I wanted to dangle all my remarkable little goodies in front of her. I wanted her hungry for every tidbit that I might share it with her completely, every twist and turn in the telling of it. It seemed to me, all the chaos of the last few days would then be justified, that this would be my reward, that the game itself would be an anticlimax if I could not share it with her.

As I picked up the phone, I was stunned by the thrust of my emotion, so much so, I failed to complete the dialing for fear of embarrassment when she answered. When I finally went through with it, it was not Pat who answered, but the cold brusque rasping voice of Lester himself.

I hung up immediately, my chest feeling splattered by a dozen bullets. That he should be in that room seemed like an obscenity. That this cherished moment should be taken from me was an oppression. It was as if Lester were cuckolding *me*. I backed away with a growing sense of fear. For the first time, I became aware that I was falling in love with her.

I felt helpless. Somehow, she would have to find a way to call me and the sound of her voice would ameliorate my pain. I would tell her. Certainly, I had to tell her, for what else could possibly mean anything? I began rehearsing romantic lines, walking the floor with them, staring at the phone, commanding it to ring. And when it did, finally, I leaped at it, jerking it to my face so rapidly, the speaker bashed my lips into my teeth. I felt all the more foolish when the caller turned out to be Neal Harkevy, the gambling screenwriter.

"Well, Gordon, how does it look to you? Still lost in the fog of all that inside poop?"

Curiously, for all my frustration, I was not unhappy with his call. I could even enjoy his pomposity, especially now.

"And you, my friend, like so many of you rich Hollywood screenwriters, are you still clinging to some nostalgic affinity for New York?"

"Aha! I see you haven't changed your silly tune."

"Not a whit," I replied.

"Well, then, one might think you'd want to have some action. . . ."

Strange, the way his voice manipulated me. Nor was I unaware of it. I was being seduced into a bet by a master, a bet I didn't want to make, never wanted to make against him or anyone else, a bet that turned my work of art into a commerce. It seemed a shame to do a thing like that—but somehow, my resistance broke down.

"All right, Neal. . . . Suppose we say $10,000."
"Is that all?"
"Right, make it twenty."
"Twenty is fine."
"The Cowboys and three points," I summarized.
" 'New York, New York,' " he sang.

If I had a moment's guilt, it quickly dissolved in a reminder of all the money he made writing those atrocious screenplays. It was almost as if I were performing an act of retribution. The Robin Hood syndrome. I was also touched with a sudden hunger to *really* reap the benefits of my handiwork. And that, too, was easy to justify, for had I not performed an extraordinary feat? Considering the enormous risks, did I not have the right to capitalize on such expertise?

It was not difficult to contact a bookie. A few phone calls to friends in New York produced a pair of reliable names. From a phone booth in a coffee shop a few blocks from the hotel, I placed an additional $50,000 on Dallas. Indeed, the New York bookmakers were pleased to accept it, so much local money was being laid on the Bulls.

The curious thing was, I was suddenly ready to bet a lot more. Having gone to a total of $70,000, it seemed logical enough that I might double that figure and come home with a significant nest egg. That I restrained such avariciousness was due mostly to caution, not from any fear of losing, but of creating suspicion. I had a cup of coffee and retreated with grace.

The reunion with Patricia would wait. A final victory celebration would make it all the more romantic.

22

Sunday

On the center circle of the gridiron, young voices were singing of bombs bursting in air. Furtively, I glanced along the line of now-naked Bull faces, helmets tucked under arms like decapitated heads, so rigid, they seemed like standing dead. A blazing sun zeroed in on me as its primary target. Light-headed, I felt myself losing balance as though the ground beneath me were tipping. Everything became misty. I supposed that I was stricken by the enormity of the drama, the Stadium, the 90,000 people around me. For all my experience, I had never been part of anything like this. Confusion had sprung from it, creating strange doubts and unrecognizable truths. (Why, for example, was Oscar Ayers suddenly wearing number 47 on his jersey instead of number 49? I had terrible problems with that until I managed to convince myself that he always wore number 47.) Everything was different today. Right from breakfast, they hadn't seemed the same club at all. I had expected a continuing wildness, no doubt exaggerated by the coming game. Instead, there had been a lugubrious silence such as one imagines of soldiers about to go to their deaths in battle. They barely ate at the pregame meal: juice, steak, eggs, salad, pancakes, whatever they wanted, but they nibbled and sipped and sat, mostly staring at their plates, fidgeting for a while, then leaving for their rooms or a cup of coffee around the pool. When one of the wives was heard laughing, heads turned as though she'd spoken an obscenity in church. I'd said nothing through it all, infected by the tension, far too nervous myself to eat. I took a few notes, more for show than for record, all the while careful not to catch the eye of either Oscar or Perry Lee. And even as they alighted from the buses at the Coliseum then pushed their way through a host of New York fans clamoring for a touch, again there was nothing, absolutely nothing, and the forty-three men and staff simply elbowed their way in, glassy eyed and pale, never breaking stride for all the clawing bodies they had to penetrate.

Nor had the locker room been more than a sanctuary from intrusion, but the setting for a still thicker layer of tension as they taped ankles and knees or sat around fumbling through the game program as they dressed.

I had come out on the field to carry footballs for the kickers in pregame warmup, then again, for calisthenics and pass drills and signals. They went through these moves, barely grunting as they drilled, sweating in the trapped heat with the huge crowd gathering above. Perhaps I was overreacting, I mused. Perhaps there was nothing odd going on, only the spin-off of my nervousness. After all, there was Ace Carter warming up in that same old red baseball cap, an old superstition he cherished. And there was Jake Kolacka doing his own routine pregame exercises to stretch his muscles, working his legs along the top of the players' bench like a ballet dancer warming up at the bar. The flashy Coley Barone was prancing down the sidelines with his usual long-legged grace. Though I'd been with the club hardly two weeks, was it not all very familiar? Wasn't this precisely what I might expect to see?

Still, it was chilling. I could not free myself of foreboding. Back in the locker room in those final moments before game time, that funereal quiescence had become downright eerie, then as they'd emerged for the introduction to the crowd, even during the ritual of coin tossing for kickoff and the lining up on the sideline, for the singing of the Anthem, not a word from any of them. Had they been drugged? Had they secretly met and passed around some superspecial vial of pills?

My ears kept ringing with the amplified blaring of those voices and what seemed like an endless confrontation with every strident line. I could hardly bear the wait, so ferocious was my anticipation of the game. This was going to be *my* day. *I* was the epicenter of all this action. There was fear, yes, but also exultation, an awareness of the vast power I was unleashing. How could I not tremble at the oncoming sounds of ". . . and the home of the brave," stretching for those final reverberating notes with childlike impatience as the crowd broke through the music in a hungry roar. The players, at long last released, suddenly let out a piercing yell that penetrated the Coliseum like the proverbial cry of Indian warriors about to attack, suddenly rushing together toward an undefined center, sweeping me into the vortex until we stood in a solid mass of grunting, heaving, growling beasts, not speaking words though saying all they needed to say. Then, breaking apart with a guttural shout, eleven of them raced onto the field.

And so began the Superbowl.

23

I would read later that there were three heart attacks (no deaths) among the 90,000 at that game. Tragic, though not surprising, really. It was the sort of day that shattered one's equanimity regardless of which team one rooted for. A seesaw game of sudden shifts, a game of startling reversals and unsurpassable suspense.

A game?

The word deceives for it suggests pastime, levity, pleasurable competition. From where I stood, this was Armageddon, a war for survival itself. If there was joy in its playing, I saw none of it, only the relentlessly taut, brutal battering of savage men. As I paced the sidelines offering wet towels and containers of Gatorade to bleeding, sweating, punch-drunk men, I struggled to understand what was happening on the field. The players' bench, they say, is the worst seat in the ballpark. I was left to scramble through the steaming sideline sprawl of movement, craning for a view of the play, sometimes standing tiptoe on the bench itself for a workable perspective, then edging toward Coach Seager in hopes of overhearing the reports of spotters from vantage points high in the stands, always frenzied beyond coping until my head was throbbing unmercifully.

The game, yes. Sixty minutes that took forever. A total of less than eight minutes of actual action, they say, a bewildering statistic that becomes completely incomprehensible—like narrowing a soldier's experience in two years of war to a few seconds of actual combat.

The game began in a satisfying pattern, like a well-constructed scenario. The Bulls moved the ball through three driving first downs, then conveniently stalled. It was a lot easier to watch Oscar in action than Perry Lee, for he roamed the defensive backfield practically alone. When he made one tackle, it was too late to contain a drive for a first down. Good going, Oscar! Eventually, we got the ball back on our own thirty, pushed into Cowboy territory and again were stopped. We punted into the end zone.

The Cowboy quarterback, Roger Staubach, began to throw the ball, hitting Preston Pearson twice, penetrating all the way to our twenty-nine yard line as Oscar crossed to make a touchdown-saving tackle. I didn't mind; I sensed it was something he was expected to do. Jud Kling then made two penetrating tackles, and Dallas ended the drive with a field goal.

Fine, I thought. We were losing and the execution had been perfectly free of taint.

This time, however, the Bulls' offense was unstoppable. Ace Carter was brilliant. Though we blasted through for long gains, moving for a touchdown barely eight plays after the kickoff, I was not dismayed. After all, I never fancied this was going to be a rout for Dallas. Nor, I reminded myself, did I really want it to be.

So the first period ended 7–3 in our favor.

And the second began in mine. Not only was the next

Bulls drive stalled short of midfield, but the Cowboys turned on a glorious assortment of power and finesse, ending with a flare pass to Newhouse as he spun out of the blocking pattern, circling out to the flank with two big linemen blocking for him. I watched Oscar abandon his deep pass coverage of Golden Richards and plunge into the action. Newhouse skirted by Wisting as the two blockers hammered at Kling to keep him out of reach, then cut sharply toward the goal line. Oscar made the cut with him, knifing across the field to hit him by the four yard line, flinging his agile body at the ball carrier in a desperate tackle that hit but not quite solidly enough to stop him from stumbling over the goal line for a touchdown. The Cowboys now had seven more points to go with the three, and Oscar had executed a thing of beauty.

Late in the period, the Bulls began a typically hard-nosed drive all the way to the Cowboys' twenty-eight; every play seemed perfectly executed: five yards, eight yards, eleven yards, a steady procession of strong penetrations. One could feel the enormous power that sustained it. It was third and one, and there was no question but that, with another first down, we would go in for another score, and the half would end with the Bulls in a substantial lead. I stood tall on the bench, my body tense, my teeth chomping on a sweated towel. I could hear Stonewall Jackson calling numbers when, suddenly, a single Cowboy lineman charged, arms flailing as he battered into Perry Lee, knocking him into the Bulls' backfield. Whistles blew, beautiful little yellow flags flew in the air and dropped, and tears of joy flooded my eyes, for the Bulls were penalized five precious yards for illegal procedure. Perry Lee had provoked it—brilliantly, to be sure, and with perfect timing. A costly penalty that would stop the Bulls' momentum. Instead of a first down with goal to go, it was third and six. Jackson was forced to throw, only to be blitzed by a linebacker and a safety, deflecting the pass directly into the hands of a Cowboy cornerback, and he ran forty yards before Ace Carter could bring him down at midfield.

A wonderful reversal, enhancing the validity of all my theories. Football is a game of momentum. Every football fan has seen it happen repeatedly: make one mistake and suddenly everything changes. Perry Lee had done that. Everyone in the ballpark knew that the Cowboys would take full advantage of their momentum.

Staubach was brilliant. With two minutes to go, he pecked away with short passes to the sidelines. Eight yards, six yards, twelve yards, and the receivers would step out of bounds to stop the clock, a steady movement toward the New York goal. There were almost thirty seconds left in the half when Newhouse ran a draw play in from the nine yard line for still another Dallas score.

I had trouble containing my joy as the half ended. It was 17–7, a fantastic Dallas lead, and I followed the despondent Bulls into the locker room with an exaltation that seemed so potent, I had to bite my lips to contain it.

What followed was a scene of such incredible madness, no one could possibly recount it without mitigating its power. I entered that steaming locker room to the sound of helmets being slammed into lockers to resound like cannon shots, voices that crackled like accompanying machine gun fire. Coach Seager and his staff retreated to the inner office after a vain attempt to contain it. Lester Stillson himself came in, haughty and defiant, shrieking over the din, his insipidly high register ringing out like the cry of a baby.

"You sonsabitches! You goddam sonsabitches!" he screamed, as though insult could achieve silence where all else failed. As it turned out, it was the straw that broke the camel's back. Stillson had hardly stopped to take a breath when a ferocious roar rose from the players, a cry of despair and fury that was terrifying in its own right. This was immediately supplemented by the body behind it, an enraged bull charge so intense, ten men could not have stopped it.

It was Jud Kling, of course, and he threw himself across thirty-odd feet of floor space, crashing into Stillson's brittle body with such power, Stillson's terrified squeak could barely be heard above the contact. Kling picked him up by his clothes, carrying him like a satchel to the door, whereupon he literally threw him out. He slammed the door behind him, locked it, then surveyed the stunned mass of players like a giant king of the gorillas. He was breathing fire now, his chest heaving with rage, his eyes passing from one to another as he began to walk around the room. No one moved, absolutely no one, then finally he appeared to see what he was looking for.

"Kolacka, you fuck!" he roared in an ear-splitting cry, the hard sound of all those k's bombarding the walls, creating eerie echoes.

Jake was stretched out on the floor not ten feet from me, his back propped against a wall, half an orange in one hand, a cigarette in the other. He looked up to see the charge, but not in time to defend himself.

Kling came at him with a vicious open-handed slap that cracked loudly across Kolacka's face, sending the orange flying off as if an ear had been severed by the blow.

"You prick, you're *doggin'* it!" Kling roared.

Jake scrambled to his feet, keeping bodies between them for a moment's protection. Cornered, he went into a linebacker's crouch waiting for Kling to come at him again. Kling wasted no more time, charging into Jake the way he attacked a ball carrier, slamming him into the lockers where he tore into him like a wild man, slugging him unmercifully until Kolacka fell helplessly to his knees, crawling away in a bloody mess. Kling towered over him, still spitting fire, and for a moment I thought he was going to stomp him, perhaps even kill him while no one moved a muscle to intercede. Then, catlike as though someone might, he whirled to face the others, his chest heaving now, his eyes flashing in the center of his ugly, filthy, battle-scarred face.

"You fucks. . . . Something ain't right out there. They got no right scoring 17. They got no right scoring shit!" His voice boomed, rattled off walls like an amplified trumpet. His fury was absolutely beyond belief. "If I smell any more o' that, I'll *kill* someone, I'll kill him right there on the field!"

For an instant, there was silence, no sound but Kling's breathing, and he moved around the room glaring at one after another, fist opening and closing as though he were debating whether to pop someone else. He merely growled as he faced them, a guttural sound that bespoke his fury. And gradually, in response, a mumbling arose from the others, one encouraging the one next to him, a rising sound like oncoming thunder. They were all on their feet, sustaining the message with more and more power, slamming fists into lockers to supplement the emotion, fury piled on fury until tears were streaming down mud-sweated faces. No longer the fury of frustration, this was the call to the hunt. Nor did they stop to let that emotion dwindle at its summit but began to tear apart the cubicles that housed their clothing, using chunks of wood to smash at the walls. And when Seager dared to announce that the half-time intermission was up, they exploded through the locker room door like the bulls of Pamplona released to run those narrow streets.

Dutifully, I followed them with my batch of towels, my head throbbing again with a fresh wave of fear. The sound alone had shattered me, and the power of the scene precluded all reason.

What could this possibly mean? For all the compacted fury, what difference could it make? Could I not actually rejoice at the thought of Stillson's incredible horror in the face of Kling's charge? Was that, too, not the result of all *my* machinations? What was Kling but a raging lion in the midst of a zoo!

Outside on the sidelines, everything seemed unreal. The appearance of Kolacka stunned me—like a man returning from the dead—and he readied himself for the second half as though nothing had happened just moments before. Across the field, the Cowboys seemed just as violent, pounding each other on padded shoulders like bulls pawing the earth before attacking. Though I could find surcease in that—just as my mind caressed the ten-point lead and the talents of my two stalwart colleagues—I was harassed by a deflating sense of helplessness.

Then the action began again, a pounding, vicious battle of titans. A battle fought in the trenches, as the sportscasters say. I could hear the thud of contact, the gut-wrenching screams of anger and pain, and when they were close to where I stood, the vile obscenities that followed every play. Minutes went by, and I was relieved by what appeared to be a stalemate. Neither team could move the ball. Two colossal defenses overwhelming the opposition. And Kling, of course, was irrepressible, hurtling through blockers, knocking down linemen as though the ball carrier was for him alone, his name reverberating through the crowd as they watched in fascination. However, if the Cowboys repeatedly failed to cross midfield, the Bulls could do little better, and I reveled in this wholly satisfying standoff as time swept gloriously by.

My mind did not rest with the stalemate, however. On offense, I kept watching Perry Lee for another demonstration of his complicity. If he could not be expected to jump offside again, why didn't he let his man get through to smother Stonewall? Why was he repeatedly popping the Cowboy tackle, driving him outside? Why was Carter able to punch through Perry Lee's side, four or five yards at a crack? And Oscar, why all that charged-up yelling, and why those two amazing pass deflections on the dead run, leaping like a kangaroo to knock down passes with his fingertips? Were they both waiting for another key moment to do their thing? *Our* thing?

I worried. Of course, I worried. The game seemed to be on fire, infecting everyone with a fury. Something was going to destroy the incredible balance. Something climactic. Would the Cowboys break the game open and run away with it? Or would the Bulls spin it around and squeak through with the victory?

Then, near the end of the third quarter, it happened. And not surprisingly, it was Kling who caused it. Staubach handed off to Newhouse on a delayed draw, but Kling hit him with such ferocity, the ball popped into the air like a cake of soap in a shower, and it settled into Kolacka's arms for a devastating interception. It was all Stonewall Jackson needed, and four plays later, the Bulls had another touchdown.

The third period ended, 17–14. The Cowboys were still ahead, but the game had definitely taken a new direction. The Bulls' sideline became a chaotic mass of moving bodies spewing endless profanities. Suddenly, there was Lester himself in his brightly colored plaid pants and pastel blazer, having left the spotter's booth for the sidelines for the first time, jumping from one group to another, shoving his sweaty red face into the endless miniconferences that dominate the constantly shifting stratagems, shrieking at this one and that, pointing his finger at face masks beyond his reach. I tried to watch my two compatriots, desperate to see what they were doing. Again, it was impossible to make judgments, and when Perry Lee came off the field as we lost possession of the ball, all I could see were glazed eyes partially hidden in the deep shadows behind the grotesque cage of his helmet. No, I didn't like the feel of it. On one play, Newhouse crashed off tackle, broke through Kolacka's grasp with a vicious spin of his body, and was able to break for at least a dozen yards when Oscar slammed into him, his taut steellike body brutally chopping Newhouse to his knees, the last man between Newhouse and the goal. Then, on another, Oscar doggedly raced halfway across the field to cover a receiver on a deep fly pattern, just managing to pop him as the ball arrived, forcing an incompletion.

Why such perfection? Oscar, Oscar, what is happening out there?

We held at 17–14 for several more exchanges, but I liked the prospects less and less. Ace Carter was running strong again. He had already passed 100 yards for the day. I hated him. I wanted to put strychnine in his Gatorade. I wanted to kick Kling in his gonads. I could feel it now. I was in deep trouble.

Finally then, Dallas began moving the ball, for the first time this half. Staubach, unable to find an open receiver, scrambled for a first down. Dennison cut off tackle for another. With second and two, Staubach passed to Pearson on a play-fake and the Cowboys were well across midfield.

Dallas fans were alive again, sustaining a relentless chant of "Go... Go... Go... Go..." and my heart began to pulse in tempo. Above it, I could hear Kling bellowing at his men as the Cowboys lined up, catching such exhortations as "Move, you yellow fuck!... Penetrate, Tiny, you lazy sonovabitch!" Or, repeatedly: "I'll kill you, I swear!" Then the play would begin and he would tear into the action, screaming at the ball carrier as though he could scare him to a halt. But the Cowboys kept gaining yardage. In three plays, they were up to their forty yard line, pouring on power directly at Kling himself. On first down, Staubach faked to Dennison into the line, then popped a swing pass to Newhouse as he circled to the right, and as Kling turned to pursue the play, four big Cowboys were waiting for him, plowed into him, smothering him in a ferocious pile-up while Rollie St. Clair drove Newhouse out of bounds fifteen yards downfield.

Incredibly, Kling did not get up. For the first time in over a hundred games of professional football, he lay on the ground unable to move. The crowd roared at the first sight of it, then fell into shocked silence as if Superman himself had been felled by a single bullet. The trainers raced out to him with Doc Knowland waddling behind, provoking fresh gasps from the crowd. When they led him off, limping badly, I could hear him shrieking above the applause of the crowd, shaking his fist at his teammates: "Kill them! Kill the fucks!" He refused to go inside for treatment, but encased his shattered knee in ice packs to watch the game on the sidelines.

Dallas had a first down again, just past midfield. The score was still 17–14, with at least six minutes to play. I was beginning to smell a victory. I could even picture Lester falling into an apoplectic fit. After six more minutes of football, I would see him simpering in defeat, his insipid moustache twitching out of control, spittle drooling from the corners of his pale thin lips.

Even as I teased myself with such extravagant images, I knew these last six minutes would be endless. Kling was replaced by a special-teams linebacker named Stoones, who hadn't started on defense this season, and everyone knew that the Cowboys would test him. Newhouse started off right tackle then cut back over the center, right at Stoones, for a long six yards. Dennison followed his own center and rolled over Stoones for five more and a first down. Newhouse knifed through the left side for four. On the next play, however, he slipped as he started a sweep, and was hit for a three-yard loss. It was now third and long yardage on the Bulls' thirty-eight, and the Cowboys lined up for a crucial play. Beside me, Jud Kling was roaring at the defense to cover the short pass, bellowing at the front four to get Staubach, his voice booming like a cannon that rattled my bones. Staubach backed into a shotgun formation for the pass play, but he never got it off: from out of nowhere, it seemed, came Oscar Ayers on a safety blitz, hitting Staubach from the blind side with the most perfectly timed tackle one could imagine.

It was a devastating play, magnificently executed by the only man on the team I had reason *not* to expect it from.

Oscar, Oscar, what are you doing!

Everywhere I went, Lester's voice seemed to follow me. As Kling hollered at the field players, Lester shrieked at those on the bench. Once, as Ace Carter came off the field after failing on third down and two yards to go, Lester grabbed his arm with such fury, he spun the great halfback around, the finger jabbing up at the face mask as he cried out: "You stink, Carter! You're a chicken-shit athlete!" At which Ace simply pushed him away, at the moment too battered to pay heed to such drivel, and he sought the comfort of a bench seat, needing rest even more than a view of the game.

There was less than five minutes left in the game when we took possession of the ball on our twenty yard line. This was the last chance, and everyone knew it. Stonewall was cool as he approached the line-up, never bothering to signal for silence as he grinned below his helmet bar. He handed off to Ace for four yards, then tossed a quick pop to Willie Jones for a first down. Then another, exactly the same. He made it look easy, all so terribly steady and sure, it was as if he'd been waiting all day for this moment. The Bulls kept moving on every play, nothing was wasted, nine yards, five yards, seven yards. Run, screen pass, sideline pass, draw. Stonewall was ignoring the moving clock as though he had all the time in the world.

Perry Lee! My God, what are you doing out there!

At the final two-minute warning, we were on the Cowboys' twenty-six yard line, and I rushed in with towels and Gatorade jars. They drank and sucked in air and snarled across the field at the Dallas defense, muttering their fury to each other: "Ram it up the nigger's ass, Ace! . . . My fist in his crotch, the fuck! . . . We'll kill 'em, we'll kill 'em!" I stood next to Perry Lee, my eyes pleading as he poured sweet fluid into his mouth. Then he saw me and scowled, and when he finished gargling, he spat the remains directly into my face!

It was clear enough, now. The presaging of doom. He, too, was deserting me, betraying me, abandoning vengeance on his hated owner, abandoning the money that would reward him. He was a fool, an absolute fool, and it made no sense at all. I retreated to the sidelines, clinging to one last chance for victory. We could be stopped for it all. We could fumble. We could be forced to settle for a field goal, thereby sending the game into overtime. My thoughts raced over the possibilities as though, by deciding on an action, I could somehow control it. But there was no time for such indulgences. On the first play, they stopped Ace on a sweep. On the next, Z carried again for only three. It was third down and a long seven, and again I felt that marvelous surge of hope that only one who had just tasted death itself could appreciate. Stonewall dropped back to pass, then suddenly handed off to Ace again on a delayed draw play, and Ace sliced off tackle into daylight, juking one linebacker, then carrying another all the way to the fifteen yard line and out of bounds.

Bedlam, again. Jackson handed off to Z and he battled up the middle for another four. On the next play, he overthrew Barone in the end zone, stopping the clock. I was shuddering again, for the last key play was coming up. It was third down and six to go, and only twenty-one seconds left in the game. If this play failed, they'd have to go for a field goal.

I stood tall on the bench, engulfed in a crescendo of yelling wherein no words were distinguishable, just a horrendous wall of thunder. I could see Stonewall's back only down to his buttocks, the helmet tops of crouching backs. I saw him pivot at the snap, then the quick left break of the pulling guards as Ace took the handoff and cut with the flow. Then I saw Perry Lee leading the run as they tore at the gathering defense, saw him fling his body at the oncoming linebacker and send him sprawling, leaving Ace the room to turn the corner and cut hard to the little white flag in the corner.

And he went across the last white line standing up.
The Bulls had won.

24

Epilogue

March persisted like a raging lion this year, and I was as sick as a dog. I'd spent most of it in and out of bed, not caring very much about anything beyond the distress to my gastrointestinal tract, a persistent head cold and accompanying bronchitis, plus a general achy malaise that seemed to devitalize all my extremities as well. It had become a winter of self-contempt, and I suffered through these dismal months in a pall of despair.

It was all of a piece. Humiliation, defeat, sickness, for the so-called perfect crime had turned into a nightmare. If I had financial problems paying off my debts, it is the measure of my defeat that this seemed infinitely the lesser part of it. One tends to shed bad memories, to relegate the morbid to some distant recess of the brain and replace it with fresh prospects. I remained trapped in the old. I simply could not free myself. It was almost as if I had not yet finished the saga.

To be sure, there was ample reason for my distress. The flow of events that had followed the game were so bizarre, it had become part of the Superbowl folklore—and a constant reminder of my folly. Television cameras had recorded it all for posterity, and because of its grotesqueness, people never tired of seeing and talking about it. I had been fascinated by this TV view of it, for I had seen the dramatics unfold with my own eyes—then, there it was again, myself included, as though someone were telling my own sordid story back to me. In time, the day became so vividly inscribed on my mind, the slightest reminder would set that inner tape rolling again.

I will never forget the sounds. It began with the sounds. Roaring crowd sounds that enveloped me, deafening me. I remembered heat. The sounds were so overwhelming, they exuded heat. Then, in the locker room the sounds were of uproarious laughter. No shouting, just laughter. Laughter so penetrating one had to laugh with it. Wild, screaming laughter; backslapping, eyeballing laughter that escalated beyond belief until it seemed to border on madness. Sounds of champagne popping, a half-dozen bottles in rapid succession, like firecrackers. Then Kling, the mighty but crippled Kling, his quickly lubricated voice no longer hoarse, more powerful than the mass of them, shrieking as though his soul was possessed as he crashed a champagne bottle directly into the lens of the nearest TV camera! It was a shot that would surely be on the cover of next years's program.

More laughter. A group of Bulls surrounded Kling, sharing champagne with him, then they lifted him high, bad knee and all, carrying him triumphantly around the room as the others shouted his name "Kling! Kling! Kling!" sounding like a giant gong striking midnight.

They were one, this team of players. One brief moment of being together, of abandoned hatreds and sullenness, of sheer exuberance and joy. They were there for each other only, and nothing else meant a thing to them.

Lester Stillson was elbowing his way among them all, bellowing self-congratulatory messages, his hands clasped over his head as though he alone had won it all. What I shall never forget was the change of sound at this entrance—a gradual diminution of noise as one after another became aware of him, one feeding the silence of the other until the only sounds came from Lester himself.

"This is my team!" he cried out, totally at ease with the new silence, indeed, he appeared to expect it of them all. "My team! My team!" and he spread his arms as if to embrace them all like a miser making love to a huge pile of gold coins.

I could sense a foreboding in the prickling of my skin. A pervasive gut reaction of such hatred, one might well have predicted his murder. Without a word from anyone, they moved in on him, surrounding him in silence, forty huge filthy uniforms preparing to eliminate a worm. It was Ace Carter who got to him first, standing over him for a moment, staring at Lester as though he were yesterday's vomit.

Lester smiled. "Great run, Ace!" and he reached out toward the halfback for a complimentary slap on the arm.

He never quite made it. Like a fencer parrying a thrust, Ace caught Lester's wrist in his big hand and held it there, immobilizing him. Then slowly, he twisted, smiling with a touch of malevolence, and Lester turned pale with the first flush of pain and fear. Down he went in response to the pressure, sinking to his knees in a babble of pathetic squeals.

There, Ace released him and the others closed in. It was an improvisation so well structured as to seem planned. They grabbed Lester and stood him up, pulled off his pastel coat, ripped off his shirt, jerked off his plaid pants. They stripped him nude, exposing his flabby little white body in a room full of giants, then lifted him high, shaking his pale buttocks before the TV cameras as they dumped him into the laundry bin. This they spun around, more and more rapidly, this way then that, sending it careening from one side of the room to the other. And when they were through with that, they laughed, all crowding around him, suddenly dousing him with champagne. Then they lifted him, bin and all, carrying him around the room like an heroic king after some glorious crusade.

"My team, my boys!" he kept shouting until they all disappeared into the shower for another ritual immersion.

Winning had made the difference. Winning, they had spared him, for there is no ecstasy comparable to victory. One touchdown less, and Lester might have been killed in there.

I did not see him after that. Weeks later, I read he'd gone to the Virgin Islands for a week or so, and I wondered if he'd taken his wife. He hadn't, I learned, and immediately sought her out.

She was polite, and cheerful enough, and appreciative of the return of the $70,000 left from the $100,000. She was also less than ardent when I tried to embrace her. We went into the living room again, but she left me on the davenport that faced Lester's portrait, opting for a solitary chair across the marble coffee table. The stereo speakers, I noted, were emitting the lugubrious sounds of a Gregorian chant.

There was no love in her eyes, and though I saw that quickly enough, I refused to accept the obvious.

"It's nice to see you again, finally," I said.

"Well, it's been a difficult week. . . ."

"For me, too. To say the least," I added.

"I'm sorry, Gordon . . ." She was apologetic, not compassionate. She avoided my eyes, and the blood began draining from my face. I suddenly felt so feeble, I had trouble crossing my legs.

"Pat . . . what's happened?"

She found a cigarette, lit it, and blew enough smoke to conceal her face from me.

"Everything . . . nothing . . . I really don't know what to tell you."

"Was it the game? I mean, the way everything turned out?" It was hard to say "winning" when I thought of it as "losing."

"Yes . . . I suppose."

"But I don't see why that should come between us."

She was staring at the ash with growing uneasiness. Like a fool, I took a big swing at the moon, knowing I could never get near it. "Pat, I want you to know how I feel. I need you."

She sighed, flicked the ash, doused the cigarette, then, with a sudden burst of courage, faced me.

"But I don't need you, Gordon," she said, eager to end it all.

Like the fool I was, I argued.

"That's not what you felt a week ago."

"I didn't understand then."

"Understand what?"

"*You*, Gordon. I'll tell you something: my husband was right about you. You can't do a thing unless everything is all set up for you. You're really a nothing. You couldn't pull off a scheme like this even if you had twice the money. It's *real*, that's why. There'd always be something you'd miss."

I didn't know what to say. I didn't come to discuss the fix, certainly not in this context. I wanted her support and her love, not cruel condemnation.

"You're a nice man, Gordon, but you can't dance."

The coup de grace, if you will. The ironies were too much for me. I could only assume she was back in the sack with Lester, for she had him now on her own terms. The humbled winner. Successful but threatened. No doubt he pretended otherwise, perhaps even bullied her, but he needed her and she knew it. Another earth-shaking outgrowth of the Superbowl victory.

So I was left with my anguish, locked in the most dangerous category of all: neither a winner nor a good loser—with only myself to fault.

Oh, I tried to rationalize. I sat at my typewriter dutifully hammering away at the book I'd contracted to write. The words added insult to all the injuries, for I had to write as though the Bulls' triumph was my own. All the while, I kept ruminating on the game and the two men who'd been my partners, for I really could not understand how it all had happened the way it did.

Why? Why? Had the project not been a beautiful one? Even in retrospect, I could not fault myself in its execution. My choices had been superb. Having viewed the game films a few times, I saw how subtly Oscar and Perry Lee had done their work in the first half, then betrayed that same brilliance in the second. It was the ultimate application of salt on the wound that Perry Lee's final game-winning block had become a classic on television for sports fans, an oft-repeated slow-motion balletlike configuration that will continue to haunt my dreams. I know, I know, my two colleagues had been swept up by the collective emotion. They'd forgotten everything to save the victory. But this was precisely what I could not fathom—such childishness, such idiotic sacrificing of the equivalent of an entire year's pay. For what? For the glory and profit of a man they despised? For the added humiliation of knowing they would only be abused and cheated by him all the more? Why? What did they gain but the right to strut around flashing that grotesque Superbowl ring!

It would take me weeks of grueling work to finish the book, pressing for a May 1 deadline my publisher needed for an early winter's release. So I struggled to pound out a story through the pall of anguish that was my lot.

Oh, it was all there for me, for I had done my homework well. A plethora of notebooks filled with zaniness. I would write a tough, amusing, informative book about a team of madmen winning a classic victory in the closing seconds. In the process, to be sure, I would make mockery of Lester Stillson with rapierlike slashes, reducing his idiot egocentricities to a proper absurdity. Had there ever been a more likely character for such an exposure? Was not such a book a shoo-in for the best seller lists? And did I not have that absolutely stirring fluvial locker room conclusion?

What more could any writer ask for?

Yet all along, something was missing. Something inside myself. Some thematic ingredient to spark me. It was as if I had collected all the colorful garments for a glittering display, but there was nobody to hold it together. A book without an adequate core, so to speak. A writer must always ask himself; what, in the deepest sense, was I trying to say?

I tried to forge ahead with the reckless abandon of a defensive lineman charging a quarterback, pretending, I supposed, that my emptiness was merely an outgrowth of my depression. Was Patricia my problem, not "The Bulls and I"? Weeks went by while I felt the dreariness of a prisoner waiting vainly for parole. I went out seldom in the wretched weather, permitted fewer friends to visit, felt no desire for the companionship of women. I found some surcease in drinking, though not to excess.

Early one afternoon, I discovered I was running out of Scotch and, failing to get a call through to my liquor store, decided to brave the elements with a three-block walk to make the purchase. It was a mistake. Though I had dressed warmly, I was immediately chilled by a brisk late March wind and was far too weak to hurry. Another reminder of my fragility. I was coughing as I made the purchase, aware of the curious stare of the merchant at my unusually pale and unshaven face. I smiled to make light of it, but he clucked nonetheless, presumably displeased at the prospect of a degenerating clientele in the neighborhood.

It was a day when I was so dependent on the Scotch, I was sorely tempted to duck into a doorway and open the bottle right there in the street. I hurried back to my apartment, only vaguely conscious of the two taxis and one sedan that pulled up to the curb in front of me. It was only when I saw them disgorge a mass of huge bodies did I recognize trouble.

There were at least ten of them. The Bulls. Black, white, offense, defense. Ace Carter, Willie Jones, Gil Warner, Etore Wisting, Tiny LaTourette, Jake Kolacka, Stoney Jackson, Gino Baletti, and, of course, Oscar Ayers and Perry Lee Stover. They were dressed in an assortment of brightly colored coats, some fur collared and cuffed; they wore boots and their hats were Russian furred or broad brimmed, all extremely flashy and high-styled. Indeed, they seemed impeccable, the way Americans expect a team of champions to look—and then some.

It was such an intimidating sight, I was completely unequipped to face it. I would have turned and ran if they had not seen me. First, the sly Kolacka, then, next to him, Etore Wisting, nudging each other with elbow jabs. I could see their incredulity at my degenerate appearance. I literally stumbled toward them, barely managing to stay on my feet. I worked at my face, trying for a respectable smile, but it must have been a travesty for they did not bat an eye.

"Jesus . . ." one of them mumbled in disgust.

"Well, hello, gentlemen," I greeted them. "What a surprise to see you all!"

They stared, breaths steaming in the chill. I found Oscar's face just long enough to catch his venom. I did not dare look at Perry Lee. What I could see was that they *all* knew, and that was surely why they had come.

It was too much for me to cope with. I felt only fear.

How long would it take them to tear me apart? Thirty seconds? A minute? Had they planned to take turns, like a gang rape?

Then another taxi pulled up with one last arrival. Jud Kling emerged, crutches first, dressed in a shining leather coat that made him seem like a wet rhino. As if on cue, then, they came at me, and my arms were encased in huge hands. Fittingly, I was escorted inside by Oscar and Perry Lee.

My apartment had often befriended as many as fifty for cocktails, but never did it seem so oppressively crowded as now. They opened their coats but did not remove them, obviously not planning to stay long. I tried to find some measure of relief in that, but failed, sinking to a chair out of sheer helplessness. A part of me simply gave way, like a wall of wet sand slipping into the rising tide.

Nevertheless, I was terrified. I cannot recall ever being so frightened. They were solidly together, every gesture reflected that. There would be no way to penetrate had I the resources to try. It was a terror enhanced by their silence, an obvious prelude to some vicious eruption. I could actually feel them getting psyched up, jaws working behind grinding teeth, fists digging into coat pockets. What would they do? What, indeed! Kling, the mighty Kling. What would *he* do! My God, who would have dreamed that it would come down to this!

Finally, it was Ace, the captain, who broke the silence.

"We had a meeting, pal. It happened because of Oscar, here. He spit up his guts. Then Perry Lee. Oh, it was something all right. Never heard nothing like it, you know? First off, we all thought maybe you ought to hear what they had to say."

Then Oscar began.

"Man, I gotta tell you, there was a whole mess of shit in my head. I mean, I came off the game all fucked up. I ain't *never* been so fucked up." His voice rose as he spoke, and he pointed his finger at me, stabbing the air in front of him. "When you gave me that big bread, I thought, well shit, what's the use. Like nothing matters, you know?" And he challenged me to say something. I didn't know why, but suddenly I began to defend myself as though this were some sort of a trial.

"Well, nothing did, Oscar. I thought you and I agreed on that. There was Stillson, the man everyone despised. You lived it, Oscar. All of you lived it. It was a way to punish him. . . ."

"NO!" he cried out. "Shit, no! That ain't it at all. What do I give the least fuck about Stillson!" His ebony skin turned surprisingly reddish. "That game, man, that was like torture. You said, have fun out there, like it was just another Sunday afternoon picnic. I took the bread, so I tried, dammit, but there ain't no fun being a fink. You can't dig, that, can you? I mean, you think, sheeit, *everything* is a fucking picnic!"

It was strange. As his voice rose, so did my need to persist, in spite of the fact that I was provoking him. Or, even more bizarre, was it *because* of that?

"Oscar, you were as big a cynic as I. You laughed at the whole thing. You loved the prospects. And don't tell me you weren't enjoying yourself that first half."

He snarled at me, his brow curling into deep lines above his shining eyes. Yet he tried to contain himself like one struggling to be reasonable.

"The trouble with you is, you don't know what it's like on that field. A football game has a life. It breathes. It has a fucking smell, even. It takes your body and beats at it. It tells you things that make you think. You *wonder* about yourself. I mean, any dude can be big with the flashy broads, but on that field is where you know how you are. You followin' me, man?"

"You should have thought of that when we talked, Oscar," I snapped, a brashness to my tone that startled even me, for I was fully aware of the potential consequences. "From where I sit, it is *I* who should be chewing *you* out. You and Perry Lee. You took my money and betrayed me!"

Such words were positively suicidal, but I didn't care. My hands made fists and my flesh was tingling. I was saying to them all, Come on, do what you came to do. I'm ready. I'm more than ready, for I suddenly realized the source of all my recent suffering: I'd been waiting for them!

"Man, you understand nothing!" Oscar barked. "That was a football game and we was football players. That's all we are. That's all we ever been. We don't know anything else. Man, that's all we got! I couldn't go through with your jazz because if I did, I'd never trust nobody again! Sheeit, I hated your fucking guts. I know you, man, you think we all a bunch of dumb assholes, and maybe we are, but I can tell you one thing for sure, *you is one big piece of shit!*"

Before I could respond, Perry Lee put the icing on the cake.

"Y'all were a serpent, Gordon. No matter that it weren't no Garden of Eden. Y'all were a serpent because you pretended to be my friend," and he shook his head at the torment of his memory.

It hurt. It hurt enough to silence me. My throat locked, so much so that I would not have been able to speak had I wanted to. I sat there waiting for their next move. Somehow, I wasn't afraid anymore. Let them do with me what they wanted.

It was up to Ace again, and he took a long deep breath as if he'd expended more energy today that he did on that final touchdown.

"We decided to have a little ceremony, pal. You know, to sort of celebrate the occasion . . ."

On cue, Oscar and Perry Lee came forward, pulling

from their coat pockets the same white envelopes I had given them. Inside, I could see the thick wads of green bills, all of which they ceremoniously emptied into my fireplace.

Behind me, meanwhile, Kolacka and Wisting of the defense, Gil Warner and Willie Jones from the offense, were at my desk, collecting every piece of manuscript paper they could find. It was all right there, of course, and in a convenient pile. They quickly recognized their names on the typescript; they also had no trouble finding the familiar spiral notebooks I'd used during my weeks with the club. All these items, they dropped in the fireplace.

"No . . ." I began to plead with them. "This is my work. You have no right destroying a man's work!"

They seemed not to hear me, especially Kolacka, who was pouring a can of lighter fluid on the large pile. I elbowed my way to the hearth, intent on stopping them at this final moment, but two huge hands lifted me back to my seat and dropped me into it.

"You gotta understand, pal," Ace explained. "We don't want your book any more than we want your money. The book is shit, the money is shit." Then he put his lighter to it and the whole thing burst into flames. "We're just burning shit," he concluded.

"Amen," said Perry Lee Stover.

"Amen," said the others.

In time, they were satisfied that nothing was salvageable. They filed out one by one until only Ace remained. He stood in the doorway for one last look at the fire, then at me. He was smiling now, obviously pleased with himself.

"So long, pal . . ." he said, and then he was gone.

When the door slammed behind him, I rose from the depths of my chair and found the Scotch in the side pocket of my coat. I opened it, poured a stiff drink, downed half of it, letting its warmth seep into my gut before I moved. Then I went to the fireplace and watched the flames curl the white pages, an occasional familiar name or phrase appearing through the blaze, remembering my torments as I had worked on it. And the money, there were half-charred remnants of a few bills still smoldering on the fringes, and I could not help but think of the marvelous erotic interplay when these very same bills were delivered to me.

I grabbed the iron poker from its stand, moving papers around to stoke the fire into a freshly roaring blaze. At the moment, I didn't understand why, but the sight of it was not without pleasure.

I got marvelously drunk that night. In my weakened condition, a quart of whisky was more than enough. I knew I could not stand up and had the sense not to try. My chin was dripping to my chest in giddy exhaustion, but my mind never lost its hold on reality. I liked that. I thought of the occasion as a celebration and not a wake, for the truth was, it was finally all over. I'd been stripped of the hair shirt. The manuscript was gone, the money with it. The infamous project was dead and buried. But above all, they'd come to deliver what I needed most: punishment.

That was the key, I realized. I did not have to suffer any longer.

For all my dissipation, there was no hangover in the morning. In fact, I felt fine immediately on awakening. Incredibly, I'd rid myself of all those irritating symptoms during the long night's sleep. Gone was the rasping cold, the bronchitis, the ever-present aches I'd been living with, miraculously, all gone. I'd been restored by a rejuvenated spirit.

For the first time in months, I ate a hearty breakfast and

enjoyed every morsel. Even the morning papers seemed alive again. I had no notion of what I was going to do, what new project I would find to work on; indeed, I had absolutely no plans. I would call my publisher with the thrust of the bad news, to assure them all of a proper substitute in due time. I would advise my literary agent of my availability. Then I would phone a few choice friends to restore the pleasures of my social life.

But first, I would reactivate my body, too long limp with depression and affliction. What I needed was a mild but exhilarating workout. A game of squash, perhaps.